Pulpit Rock Press, Reno, Nevada

Cover Illustration by Blazey Design
43 Horsehoe Drive
Chicopee, MA 01022

Editing and text layout
by Barbara Robidoux of Word Pro
127 Gelinas Drive
Chicopee, MA 01020

Printing by St. Charles Place
Springfield, MA

Published by Pulpit Rock Press
7621 Diamond Pointe Way
Reno, Nevada 89506

First Printing: 1997
Second Printing: 1998
Third Printing: 2001

Library of Congress Catalog Card Number:
97-92420

ISBN 0-9659274-0-7

*This is dedicated with affection
to the DeJong family
without whose charity, courage,
and goodwill I would not have lived
to be able to tell this story.*

Faye Adam

Prologue

My name is Faye Adam. I was born at my maternal grandparents' house in Wupperthal, Germany on a cold January 10 in the year 1932. My parents, Rose and Ernest Adam, named me Felicitas, but then quickly nicknamed me Felie (Feelee).

The events I am about to relate to you happened in Holland in World War II. My story is not unique. Thousands of Jewish children had similar experiences, some better some worse than mine. Each story of those years under Nazi rule is important. The record must remain.

Map by DONNA BLAZEY

Chapter 1

I don't remember life without fear. Perhaps it began when I was a baby being cared for by a nurse rather than my mother. Or maybe the first tinge of fear arrived when as a toddler I watched Mother dress for work and knew she would be leaving me. Or is fear my genetic legacy? Does it come from being born into a race that has been driven from country to country to country, never feeling settled or secure? I don't know. But I do know my life has been lived within the shadow of anxious thoughts and fear-filled dreams. Even today I'm afraid to worship in public or to wear jewelry with the Star of David on it, and I still look over my shoulder in dread at people who I'm not sure can be trusted and at a world that seems full of cruel surprises.

The fear may have taken hold in 1933 when Adolph Hitler seized power in Germany. Although I was too young to remember, I'm sure the atmosphere around me must have changed then. Grandfather and Grandmother Karafiol (I called them Opa and Oma) would have felt the stress of the times. They had faced persecution before. Oma used to tell me about how happy she was when she and Opa were newly married and living in Russia where they built a successful business and had many friends.

"But then we had to leave our friends and move to another country because of some bad people," she would tell me. Then she would ruffle my curly hair in love and change the subject. But each time she told the story, she always ended it with the admonishment, "Be a good girl, Felie, bad people make good people cry."

When I was older, I found out that Oma and Opa had fled from Russia because of an organized massacre of Jews called a pogrom. They resettled in Warsaw, Poland where they learned Polish and established another business. A daughter, born to them there in 1903, died as a toddler after falling from a table. Paul was born in 1905, and my mother, Rose, arrived in 1908.

When my mother was two, Oma and Opa were forced to leave Warsaw to escape another pogrom. They moved to Dusseldorf, Germany where, over time, they learned to speak German and established another business. Three more children were born there: Toni, Ida and Sabina.

The family enjoyed a few years of security before the only too familiar undercurrents of racist speech and political conditions began to rise up. Opa knew we could soon be facing the threat of persecution so he began to make plans for us to leave our prosperous life behind and begin life over again in another strange country.

On the other hand, my father's parents—they were always Grandfather and Grandmother Adam to me—had a much easier life. They were of German origin and financially well off. My father was born in 1897 and a brother and sister followed. In the late 1920s, when my father finished his schooling in Germany, the family sent him to the United States where he settled in Boston, Massachusetts and began to study to be a doctor. Unfortunately, those ambitious career plans were abruptly interrupted when Grandfather Adam became ill and my father was called home to take care of the family.

At that same time, my mother was about to accept a marriage proposal from a young man who was planning to go to Argentina to live. When she told my grandfather of her plans, he was so upset that he sat shivah—a mourning period of seven days observed after the funeral of a close relative. After watching her beloved father cry over her impending leaving and listening to him express his grief over the loss of his favorite daughter, my mother called off her engagement plans. Opa was pleased and within a very short time he had arranged a marriage between his daughter and my father, "the nice young man who had come home from America." The couple were married on May 15, 1930, and a proud and happy father took his hand-picked son-in-law into the family business and treated him like a son. I still wonder if my mother ever loved my father or if she pined for her lost love for her whole life.

I was born in 1932 and a year later Adolf Hitler came to power in Germany. Soon his Nazi party proclaimed that the Jewish people would be singled out for harsh treatment. First our shops were boycotted and then we lost our jobs and our civil rights. We had to declare the value of our possessons, and were bullied by civil service workers. The police often arrested us and forced us to sell our property for much less than it was worth.

Opa told the family it was time to begin to secretely close out the affairs of the furniture stores we owned—one in Dusseldorf and the other in Wupperthal. "We'll move our families to Holland," he told the men, "then we'll sell off our assets a little at a time and smuggle the money out of Germany."

Holland was known for its religious tolerance and neutrality during World War I, so, when we finally made our move, we joined thousands of other Jewish refugees who were streaming into what we all thought would be a safe country.

For the first year my mother and I lived with Opa and Oma in Diemen, Holland. Then we all moved to Amsterdam where Opa and Oma settled on the Stadionweg near the Beethovenstraat. Mother rented a large, three-room apartment a few blocks away on the Panasassweg. My father was still in Germany finishing off the final business matters, but Mother assured me he would soon be joining us in our new home.

Like most of the citizens of Amsterdam, we lived in a tall, narrow apartment which was part of a block-long brick building. An orange slate roof sloped above lace-curtained windows at both the front and back of our apartment. Window boxes held plants and seasonal flowers. The building faced a cobbled street lined with poplar trees. I used to love listening to the pigeons and seagulls as they swooped around the city. I remember taking walks with Opa and going by stores full of stylish clothing. Open markets offered foods and flowers that we would sometimes buy to bring home to Oma. People usually traveled by bicycle, but in the winter even the adults would put on wooden skates and skim along the canals.

Mother seemed to adjust to her new life in Amsterdam fairly well. She made friends easily and soon was busy with her social schedule. At the end of two years, my father finally tied up all the loose ends of the business and was ready to leave Germany. Unfortunately for him and for us, when he crossed into Holland he was arrested and put in a Dutch prison. He was charged with bringing monies into Holland without proper documentation and for not paying taxes. This violation of Dutch law made him individually responsible for a crime the whole family had committed.

Of course, I missed my father and was quite envious of the neighborhood children who had their fathers at home. My mother rarely hugged or kissed me or showed me any affection. I especially hated eating the evening meal because I always ate it alone staring at the wall while Mother busied herself with her own affairs. Fortunately, my grandparents made up for the love missing in my home. I was their first granddaughter and they doted on me.

When he was young, Opa had lost sight in one eye due to a skiing accident. When he turned fifty-five the good eye deteriorated. He was declared legally blind and could no longer work but he managed to keep active partly due to a beautiful white Samoyed dog named Prince who was always at his side.

I loved Wednesdays! We would have a half day of school at the Montessori school where I was enrolled. Opa and Prince, my two companions, would pick me up about noon. My heart skipped a beat when I saw them waiting for me; it skipped two beats when Opa dug into his pants' pocket and pulled out five cents for me to spend at the nearby candy store. It would take me at least ten minutes to look over all the treats before I finally picked my favorites—penny candies and brightly colored gum balls that changed color as they melted in my mouth. I would clutch this bag of treasures as I skipped along beside Opa and Prince all the way home to Oma who would have scrambled eggs, home fries, and small green peas ready for us. That lunch is still my favorite today.

Chapter Two

In March of 1938 when I was six, Hitler's forces marched triumphantly into Vienna, Austria. I remember hearing Mr. Cousins, our neighbor from upstairs, telling my mother about how the Nazis were treating the Viennese Jews. "Those poor people had their possessions taken from them and were forced to clean out public toilets and scrub the streets," he raged. "Somebody should stop this foolishness!"

Mother agreed and told the family about it when we gathered around Oma's dining room table that night for dinner. The adults were shocked. Later they heard reports of more such atrocities being taken against Jews throughout all of Europe.

The most disturbing case of persecution for us at that time happened on what is now called Kristallnacht (Crystal Night or "the night of the broken glass") when Jewish people in Germany were violently attacked and their synagogues and homes vandalized and burned. My father's sister, her husband and their two daughters were murdered during a Friday evening service at their synagogue. Soon after, my uncle Herman, his wife Edna and their daughter Karen took my paternal grandparents and left Germany. They resettled in Peru, South America where Grandfather Adam lived to the age of 96, and Grandmother Adam lived to 94.

I'm sure the adults in Amsterdam were horrified by our family's loss on "Kristallnacht", but at the time I was more interested in a trip my mother and I were planning to take to Brussels, Belgium to see my Aunt Toni who was expecting a baby. We were bringing her my outgrown baby clothes. As a six-year-old, I tingled with excitement at the prospect of such a trip. Toni lived in a large brick house with beautiful gardens and flowers. She had a nanny already living with her so the woman could get used to the family's routine before my new cousin arrived.

One afternoon, when Aunt Toni and Mother went shopping for baby furniture, they left me with this nanny. After a while, the woman received a telephone call from her boyfriend that upset her. She rushed from the house completely forgetting I was playing in the back yard. When I went inside and found no one there, I ran through the house and out the front door slamming it behind me. I was locked out! A police car on patrol drove by as I sat on the front steps waiting for Mother to return. When the policeman drove by again later, I was still there. He stopped and asked, " Is everything all right?"

I couldn't understand the Flemish language, so I didn't answer him. He took me to the police station where they gave me a lollipop while they hunted down the owner of the house. Uncle Siegbert rushed to my rescue. He felt so bad for me that he took me to the largest toy store in town and let me pick out any toy I wanted before we went home. When Mother and Aunt Toni returned, I got scolded for going outside the house and locking myself out. I didn't feel I deserved such harsh words, but at least I had an adventure and a toy to remember. The nanny, on the other hand, was fired on the spot when she returned.

When Mother and I arrived back in Amsterdam, Oma reported that the war rumors had gotten worse. Everyone was afraid Hitler would invade Holland in spite of its proclaimed neutrality. Soon neighborhood air raid shelters were set up and wardens instructed us on black out rules. When Denmark and Norway were invaded in April of 1940 we practiced air raid drills weekly with a sense of impending doom amidst the wonderful smells and sights in a city full of blooming tulips, hyacinths and daffodils.

My fondest memories of those times are of the nights when Mother would go out to play cards and I would sleep overnight cuddled in between Oma and Opa under a warm down blanket. In the morning, when I woke up, Opa and Prince would be gone for their morning walk, but I would stay snuggled in so I could watch Oma at her corner vanity in front of her large oval mirror. A wooden form would be on the vanity in front of her, like the one people use now to hold their wigs. While I watched, Oma would take one of her many hats and sit there rearranging the trimmings, bows and veils to make the hat look like new. Then she would steam the felt cap over a kettle of hot water to change its shape. Later she would wear this new creation to her afternoon bridge club. Sometimes I was allowed to go with her and, when the ladies complimented her on her new hat, Oma would wink at me over our shared secret. This art of making a new creation out of something old was passed along from Oma to her daughter. It helped my mother support us after the war.

When Oma and I didn't go out, we would have a tea party in the afternoon. We always used the Russian teapot that she treasured. It had traveled with her from Russia to Poland to Dusseldorf and now Holland. The teapot was called a "samovar" (we pronounced it "shenowah") and was made out of silver. It looked like a large urn. On the bottom was a little handle like a faucet. When you put your cup below it, a strong extract of tea poured out. Oma would add boiling water to this extract and we would have our tea. The custom, when she was a little girl in Russia, was that the tea would be served with lemon and a lump of sugar in a glass mug with a handle, so that's how we had ours. The tea party was complete when Oma brought out a plate of her homemade sugar cookies.

Oma's recipes were fabulous! About one week before the Jewish holidays she would begin to prepare festive dishes for the whole family. We all especially appreciated her gefilte fish that was prepared from a Polish recipe that had been handed down from her mother. It called for two types of fish and some sugar to make it a little sweeter. My Aunt Sabina took the recipe to America and passed it on to her two daughters where it is still enjoyed today. Oma taught me to make a delicious apple cake which to this day is my family's favorite dessert, and her noodle pudding is so good that when I make it my grown children say, "It's to die for."

When cherries were plentiful in the spring, Oma would buy lots of them and remove the pits with her hairpin. Then she would put the lush red fruit in a big glass jar with a small neck opening and a wide bottom. She would add sugar and close the lid. Every few days I was allowed to shake the jug. I loved this job because I knew that after a few weeks the concoction would become the base for a delicious cherry jubilee served over Oma's pound cake.

For a child who ate most of her meals alone, holiday meals with the whole family together were treasured. Opa sat at one end of the large dining room table and Oma at the other. For as long as my father was in prison, there was an empty chair next to Opa. My uncles would sit one next to Opa and the other next to the empty chair. Then would come Aunt Toni and Aunt Letty who was Uncle Paul's wife. Mother would sit on one side of Oma and I would be on the other side. Aunt Ida would sit next to me. We always took these same seats when we gathered together around Oma's table.

After I drank a little wine with Challah bread and filled my stomach, I was allowed to leave the table and snuggle down on the leather couch in the living room. From there I listened to the grownups talking and soon fell asleep. Later, one of my loved ones would carry me to bed and I would enjoy another sleepover at my grandparents' house.

On the Wednesday afternoons I spent with them, my mother would usually come and take Oma shopping while I stayed at home with Opa. Prince and I would play while Opa snoozed in his big leather chair. I thought it was quite funny when he would tell Oma he hadn't slept a wink while she was gone. The truth was that I had usually spent most of the time sitting next to him watching him snore. What a delight it was when he would finally wake up ready to play hide and seek with me.

Dutch people celebrate St. Nicholas Day on December 5th with a traditional holiday celebration that encompasses all religions. We children loved it. The tale is that St. Nicholas arrives from Spain in a boat and sits on a big white horse along with his helper, Zwarte Peter (Black Pete). On St. Nicholas Eve, children put their shoes next to their entrance doors. If they have been good, the next morning they find their shoes filled with candy. Gaily-wrapped toys and presents sit by the fireplace. Good children are also given chocolate in the shape of an initial. My first name began with the letter "F", so I always looked forward to biting off the middle of the "F" and eating one small piece of the remaining letter each day. I was told that a child who misbehaved during the year received black soot from Zwarte Peter, but I never knew anyone who did. I do remember Mother warning me—and more than once I'm sure—that if I didn't behave she was going to put me on Zwarte Peter's list.

On May 10, 1940, the loud explosion of gunfire and the thunder of airplanes jostled me awake and changed my life forever. Sirens wailed, doors slammed and people screamed as Mother rushed into my room and pulled me from my bed.

"Hurry, Felie," she urged. "We must get to the shelter."

We ran out the door and down the street. Soldiers, tanks, and trucks were dropping from the sky under billowing parachutes. Dead bodies dangled from many of them, evidence that the German invaders were being shot at as they floated down.

As Mother dragged me along she kept saying, "Don't look up, Felie. Don't look up."

But I couldn't help it. My eyes were glued to the gruesome sight of those dead paratroopers. The smell of gunpowder and smoke enveloped us as Mother ran and I, coughing and choking, stumbled along beside her. Finally we pushed our way into the shelter in a building at the corner of the street that housed a florist and a bicycle storage area. I often rode my bike and played hide and seek near there. A sub-basement was below ground level where, for hours, we crammed into a room with about three hundred other people, mostly women and children. Three or four people huddled together in a space large enough for one. There was little talking as each ear strained for the sounds outside. The cry of a baby or whine of a toddler seemed to echo in the semi-silent room.

After a time, the whispered questions began: "What's going on out there? Can you hear them coming?

What if they find us here? Will they shoot us all?"

As soon as I could, I left Mother's side and moved close to the doorway so I could try to see what was happening outside. A tall man blocked my view, so I peeked through his legs but I still couldn't see much. Finally, after what seemed forever, the all-clear sirens sounded. I pushed past the man and rushed outside. The adults were curious but not quite as foolhardy as I was. Those closest to the door cautiously moved outside. When they didn't return, the rest pushed forward in a passionate rush to the outside and fresh air.

Mother soon found me and pulled me along until we reached home where she quickly pulled the shades and turned on the radio. Most of the fighting was taking place at Arnhem where the German invaders were meeting strong Dutch resistance. At Rotterdam, the largest Dutch seaport, our ships were being completely destroyed. The newsmen assured us the fighting would last only a few days and that our Dutch resistance would stop the invasion.

During the next few days everyone in the neighborhood crowded into the butcher shops, bakeries and greengroceries to buy extra food. The movie houses, theaters, schools, offices, and many stores were closed. No mail was delivered, and only hospitals and military personnel were allowed to use the telephone. When not out stockpiling supplies, we stayed in our homes waiting for a broadcast from Queen Wilhelmina. After a few days of what proved to be false hope, the dreadful news was announced. The queen, her family and the cabinet members had escaped from The Hague (the Dutch seat of government) and fled to London aboard British warships. They planned to rule in exile.

On May 14, Rotterdam was bombed. Nine hundred people were killed, thousands injured, and 78,000 were homeless due to fires that destroyed 750 city blocks. Holland surrendered the next day. The Germans were in full control.

One of the first things they did was issue a proclamation: *All young men between 18 and 21 years must register at the German Headquarters for the Army.* The Germans expected ready compliance, but instead large numbers of the young men fled to England or Canada while others went underground in Holland rather than serve. Only about one percent of the Dutch men answered the call to arms. Within six months, German soldiers were riding through our streets with megaphones announcing it was now a criminal act not to join the German army. Those caught would be punished.

In June of 1940, we citizens were forbidden to display the Dutch flag, the national colors, or pictures of the royal family. July brought even more restrictions. We couldn't legally listen to any radio station except the official one that controlled the news and only played German music. Mother and I soon joined most of our neighbors as we all huddled behind our closed doors secretly tuning the radio into a Dutch station broadcasting from England. Since the newspapers were not allowed to print anything negative about Germany, we heard that Dutch printers were using their small presses to print underground newspapers telling about the true progress of the war and giving advice on how to deal with the Nazi oppressors.

But, even though life around me was unsettled, when school began in September my daily routine was once again a familiar one.

Then the winter of 1940–41 arrived.

Chapter 3

In the late days of 1940, rationing coupons were issued and we immediately noticed the change in our diet and lifestyle. The Germans were exporting tons of coffee, tea, cocoa, butter, milk, vegetable oils, produce and meats to Germany. They were rationing some foods and all cloth goods. If we needed to buy socks or underwear, we had to give up buying pajamas, blankets or household items. Special permits were required for shoes and winter coats. Since Dutch coal was being shipped to Germany, we had to use gas and electricity. But, soon the Nazis restricted them, too. Then whole forests surrounding the city disappeared as people chopped down trees to burn for fuel.

Since I was now eight, Oma would often send me to the store for bars of soap or bags of sugar. I would wait in line for hours and often come home empty handed. When I complained about these hardships, Oma would tell me how much it was like what she had gone through as a young girl during World War I. I would feel better after Oma's stories because I was convinced if she could survive such hard times, I could too.

After she heard the radio announcement that all Jews in Amsterdam must register with the census office, Oma grew silent. I missed her quick and catchy laugh. I didn't know what had happened, but I knew it wasn't good! Then in February, we heard that some Nazis had attacked Jews living in South Amsterdam. This was too close for Oma. It was time for our family to take action. She called everyone together and advised them to hide any items of real value they owned such as original oil paintings, jewelry, china, silverware. My uncle insisted that Oma was overreacting. He assured her that she and Opa were safe because they were White Russian Jews, but Oma wasn't to be "put off."

It was an exciting time for me as it was my job to help her hide stuff. Since I was light and agile, I could easily climb to the attic and hide items Oma would hand up to me. We wrapped expensive oil paintings in wallpaper and tacked them to the attic ceiling and hid the silverware and crystal between the beams.

After working with Oma on this project, I realized I had something I needed to hide. It was a very special gift Mother had given me that Hanukkah. I had gone to bed early that night, but I lay awake listening to her setting up my presents on the table. I finally drifted off to sleep. The next morning I woke up to find a beautiful black box lined in blue velvet with a shiny silver artist's compass nestled in it. I loved to draw and now here I was with such a beautiful and grown-up gift! So, when Oma began hiding the valuables, I decided my treasured compass deserved a better hiding place than the attic. I brought it to my best friend, Juliat, for safekeeping until after the war. Juliat was a Gentile school companion and neighborhood playmate. She seemed pleased that I was trusting her and promised to take good care of my compass.

In May of 1941 vehicles rode up and down our streets with loudspeakers proclaiming—*All Jews over the age of five must wear a yellow Star of David with a brown outline and the word JOOD printed in black across the center. Sew the star on the chest of your clothes so it remains visible at all times.* After Mother sewed the star on my clothes, wherever I went, people stared! I was ashamed. Mother said she felt like a second-class citizen.

Even our friends and neighbors avoided us because they were afraid to be called *Jew lover.*

As spring approached, conditions got worse. We had even less to eat and what you could buy cost more. Dutch milk was being shipped to Germany, so we were allowed only one watered–down cup a day for adults and two cups for children. Cream could only be had by doctor's prescription. Most of the dairies closed and we were only allowed one egg per week. Many people turned to the Black Market for bread, meat, eggs, milk, butter and oil.

Life was tough for everyone, but especially for Jews. In June, the adults were ordered to have a large "J" stamped on the identification cards they always carried with them. Then, in August, Jewish children were banned from the public schools and ordered to attend newly–formed Jewish schools. Some of my friends had been going to a private Jewish school already, but my mother was not as religious as their parents were. She had enrolled me in a Montessori school that I loved. But now my Gentile classmates and I would no longer be allowed to study and play together.

I was assigned to a new Jewish school quite a distance from our home. It was a long walk for me, but—since the Germans had also proclaimed that Jews could only ride in the rear of buses and trolleys and only if they stood up all the way—I preferred to walk to school and back. I despised that school! I hated it so much that I would walk home and eat lunch alone every day because I hadn't yet made friends there and the unpleasant aroma in the lunchroom made me feel sick. Most of the children would bring hard–boiled eggs or salami sandwiches for lunch and, since there was no refrigeration available, the room reeked.

The walk home at noon would leave me with only about ten minutes in which to eat before I had to start back. In the winter the trip seemed shorter because I would take my ice skates and skim along on the canals. We were not allowed to bring skates into school, so I would hide mine under the bridge in the snow and hope that no one would find them there before the school day was over. The only good memory I have of this school comes from the autograph book full of children's poems and funny sayings that I was able to save. I have never been able to find even one of the forty children who signed my book. I fear none of them survived.

On December 7, 1941 our hopes were raised when the United States entered the war. The BBC also reported encouraging news from Russia, where Hitler's troops had been held back by a snowy, cold, and muddy winter. But that news didn't help the citizens of Amsterdam; in fact, it made things worse. We were ordered to turn in our coats, hats, blankets and gloves so they could be sent to German soldiers at the eastern front. Then we heard that Hitler was planning to kill all Jews. Of course, nobody believed that rumor; it was too outrageous.

Since our savings account was dwindling quickly, Mother decided to take in a boarder to help with expenses. I liked the man. He was a tall, warm and friendly Jewish gentleman in his mid fifties who had never been married. He told me to call him Uncle Siegmund (Zeekman). Even though I missed my father, Uncle Siegmund's presence made life at home much nicer. He loved to eat with us and play games with me. We became like a family.

Uncle Siegmund had some successful diamond and clothing manufacturing businesses. Since he was smart enough to realize it would only be a matter of time before the Nazis would confiscate those business holdings, he sold them to his secretary, a Gentile who had worked for him for over twenty years. The plan was that she would turn the businesses back to him after the war ended. Most of the money received from this sale was hidden in Switzerland, but some of the gold and diamonds remained in Holland in her keeping to be used for Siegmund's family and mother and me. These funds were what kept us all going through the war and opened the door to my escape.

In early July, Mother told me that Father was being released from prison and would be coming home. On the day he was to arrive, I sat in the window from early morning waiting for him. Finally, when it was near darkness, I saw him coming around the corner of our street. He looked much thinner than I remembered, and shorter. I guess my perspective had changed from my toddler picture of him to what I now saw from my ten-year-old point of view. I rushed down the stairs, two steps at a time to meet him at the door. After much hugging and kissing, I pulled him upstairs to Mother. Although she seemed a little reserved, Mother hugged him, too. In much too short a time, I was sent off to bed. Father told me he would see me again in the morning, and I fell asleep with that thought tucked snuggly into my heart.

I jumped out of bed the next morning and rushed to my mother's room expecting to see Father in her bed. Mother was alone.

"Father and I are getting a divorce, Felie," she told me. "We have been apart for much too long. Uncle Siegmund and I are going to be married as soon as the war is over."

I couldn't believe it! A ten-year-old doesn't understand such news even if prepared for it. But, to have it sprung on me on the heels of yesterday's joy was almost too much to bear. Mother told me that Father was staying in a nearby hotel. "He will come for you later," she assured me.

I waited most of the day for him. Finally, he sent word to Mother that he had found a small room in an apartment building nearby. He would come for me on the weekend and take me to the park. What a disappointment! But Mother never tolerated whining, so I smothered my pain and spent the rest of the week anxiously waiting for word from Father about his plans for our weekend together.

Friday passed, then Saturday, then finally, on Sunday, he arrived carrying a small attache case. "I'm going to sell barbershop shaving brushes, cream, and other supplies," he announced as he opened the case so I could play with the samples while he talked with Mother. Then he asked if I would like to take a walk with him so he could show me his room in the apartment complex not too far from us.

I skipped along beside him chattering away and asking what must have seemed like a million questions when suddenly, about four blocks from Mother's apartment, he stopped short, grabbed my arm, spun me around, and slapped me across the side of my face. My ear and cheek burned as I reeled from the shock.

"What have I done?" I gasped.

"That's for what you did to me when I was in prison," he growled. "I've been waiting for a long time to give you that."

I couldn't believe it! How could I have done anything to harm him when I didn't even know where his prison was? As we continued along with my sniffles half smothering his words, he told me about a letter I had sent him once. In my enthusiastic innocence, I had ended it with the words, *hope to see you soon.* The German censors in the Dutch prison interpreted that as a signal indicating Father was planning to escape. They quickly placed him in solitary confinement for six weeks. The thought of such an injustice still made him angry. Unfortunately I got the brunt of his rage.

Father remained in Amsterdam for only about five or six weeks before he was arrested again. Since his last name was *Adam*, he was on the top of the German's list. We heard that he was going to be sent to a work camp for Jews only. The morning after we were told this, I skipped school and went to stand on the sidewalk across the street from Gestapo headquarters. The crowd of men being sent to the work camp that day were gathered in the fenced-in yard of the school building. When Father noticed me standing across the street, he frantically motioned at me to go away. I never saw him again.

A few days later, loud thumping noises came from the apartment above us. Mother and I huddled together in total silence. The Cousins family lived upstairs and their eighteen-year-old son seemed to be the parents' only joy in life. Thundering bootsteps on the stairs and hysterical crying made it obvious that the Gestapo had come for the boy.

"I will see you soon, Hans," the mother screamed. But it was the last time any of us ever saw or heard of him.

After Hans's arrest, Oma called the family together on a Friday evening in September of 1942. It was time to go into hiding. Mother's older brother, Paul, and his wife decided to go to Den Haag where his wife's family owned rental property where they could hide. Paul insisted that Oma and Opa could safely stay in Amsterdam because as White Russians they were not slated for removal. Since Opa wasn't working and Oma planned to stop socializing, he felt that if they kept a low profile in the apartment on the Stadionweg it would be enough to keep them out of the German's range of interest. On the other hand, since Mother was a Polish-born Jew and I was German-born it was important that we find a place to hide until the war was over.

When we left Opa and Oma that evening, Oma gave me an extra large hug. "Take care of your mother for me, Felie," she said.

"I will, Oma," I chirped. "See you on Wednesday."

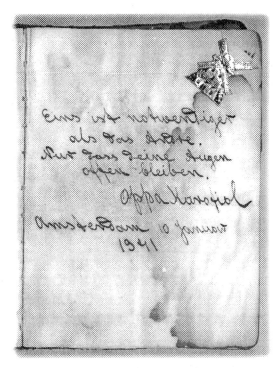

The most necessary
thing in life is
that your eyes
always stay open.
– *Oppa Karafiol*

Chapter 4

At 5:30 a.m. on a beautiful day in late October of 1942, Mother woke me. "We have to eat a quick breakfast and leave," she said. Half-asleep, I stumbled out of bed and began to dress.

"Put on two of everything," she instructed. "Two pairs of socks, two undershirts and underpants, two blouses, and two pairs of pants."

She hurried me into the kitchen where we ate toast and warm milk. Then she handed me a small pair of scissors and told me to take them with me. We left our dishes on the table as if we planned to come back. Then we put on our coats. Mother stood for a moment looking slowly around the room. At 6:00 a.m. we walked out the door. The sun was just coming up and the day seemed fresh and clean.

We only walked a short distance until we entered another neighborhood where we weren't known. Mother suddenly nudged me into a small, dark corner of a bulding. "Give me the scissors," she said. I took the scissors from my pocket and handed them to her. Then I watched with astonishment as she cut the Jewish star from my coat and hers. I couldn't believe how much freer I felt without that mark of shame on my chest.

We walked for three or four miles until we came to a neighborhood I didn't recognize. Mother found the address she was seeking and rang the bell. A woman answered and took us to a room in the attic. It had a regular-sized bed for Mother and a small floor mat for me. This was our home for the next three months. We weren't able to leave it day or night, and we had nothing to do there but to sit still and be quiet. We couldn't flush the toilet or move around because the tenants living below us would get suspicious. Sometimes the silence would make me hear noises in my head that wouldn't go away for hours; at other times I was so close to screaming I had to stuff my pillow in my mouth to keep the noise from escaping. Fortunately, Mother showed me how to embroider with thread she had made from old curtains and bed linens. Such busywork helped a little.

Soon after we arrived, Mother began to start the day by vomiting. Each morning for about a week or so she was sick. Finally, one dark night, the lady who was hiding us took her to a doctor she knew could be trusted. I spent what seemed like an eternity sitting alone in a corner of our tiny attic room hunched over in terror, praying that Mother would return. When she did, she told me, "I saw Dr. Guckal, Felie, a nice lady doctor. She told me we are going to have a baby."

I was pleased but concerned. Although Mother tried to make it seem like a wonderful thing, we both knew it was a terrible time to be pregnant! Our attic hideout wouldn't hold us all and a crying baby would surely bring the Gestapo down on our heads. Sleep came slowly that night as we tried to figure out in our own minds how we could possibly keep a baby quiet so we wouldn't all be captured.

Hoping the war would be over before the baby arrived, Uncle Siegmund asked Mother to go into hiding with him. "Felie can go to live with the DeJong's in DeZilk (de silk)," he told her. "It's a small town in the country between Amsterdam and Hillegom."

The De Jongs were the parents of the young couple with whom Uncle Siegmund and his brother Max were hiding in the city. "They have a daughter who will soon marry a teacher in DeZilk. Felie not only will be safe with these wonderful Christian people, but the teacher can provide her with books so she doesn't fall behind on her schoolwork." Mother must have thought this was a good idea for, before I knew it, Uncle Siegmund had made arrangements for his former secretary to pay a fixed amount of guilders per month plus expenses to the DeJongs in DeZilk.

Needless to say, at first I was most distressed with these arrangements. I certainly didn't want to be separated from the family and I didn't even know the people they were sending me to. But when Mother assured me I would be able to visit her and Uncle Siegmund at least once each month, my thoughts turned positive. It would be good to get out of the tiny attic where we had been confined for the last three months. And having a new brother or sister was a dream come true, for I had always wished for one. *Maybe this will be fun,* I thought. *Uncle Siegmund and Mother wouldn't send me to a bad family. And they promised I can come to visit them.*

But such positive thinking was quickly replaced by panic when it came time to leave. "You look just like a little Dutch farm girl, Felie," Mother assured me as she handed me a brown paper bag that held a water jar, a hunk of bread and some fruit. "With your blond hair and freckles the Nazis will never think you're a Jew."

Unfortunately, Mother wasn't as lucky. She had what was considered typical Jewish coloring, so she couldn't leave the attic to take me to the train. With last minute instructions and a quick hug, she pushed me out the door. I was on my own! I walked toward the train station with my favorite doll cradled in my arms. She became my only link to home and my childhood for quite some time.

I was again wearing two sets of clothing under my frayed winter coat. I didn't mind the extra bulk because I was shivering with fright as I scurried through the streets with my eyes searching ahead of me for German uniforms. I reached the station without problem and was glad I wasn't carrying luggage. Most of the other families waiting for the train were carrying paper bags, too.

When the train chugged into the station, I remembered the instructions Mother had given me and searched for a family with lots of children. When I found one, I sat as close as I could to them so it would look like I was part of the group. While I waited for the conductor to come and punch my ticket, I was shaking so hard I was sure the German soldiers who were sitting in seats all around me would certainly notice.

The conductor came and spoke to the father of the family I was sitting with, then he punched my ticket without even really looking at me. It's a good thing he didn't because if he had asked one question I would have dissolved into tears or vomited. To settle my nervous stomach, I opened my brown paper bag and gobbled up several chunks of bread.

The train ride seemed very long, and with each mile I became more anxious. *What if the farmer isn't at the bus stop to meet me? What if he meets me, but doesn't want me to stay? What if a German soldier stops me and asks what I'm doing?* My mind raced in tune with the clickety clacking wheels of the train as my child heart cried out for my mother. I never asked why Mother didn't bleach her hair and leave with me at night through the underground route. It just seemed more important for her to stay in Amsterdam with Uncle Siegmund than to be with me in the country.

The train finally pulled into the station in the small town of Haarlem. Mother had told me to get off there and take the bus to DeZilk. The train stopped, I got off, the bus was there, and I got on. Things were going just as planned. The driver asked where I was going and soon we were on our way to my new home. About half an hour later, the bus stopped in front of a small, white church and the driver said, "Here we are little girl. DeZilk. Is someone meeting you here?"

"My uncle will be here soon," I answered. "I'll be fine. Thank you."

The bus chugged off and I was alone. Mr. DeJong hadn't arrived and my thoughts raced as I tried to plan what I would do if he never came. I was too afraid to go into the church, so I sat on the front steps facing an old cemetery next to the building and waited. After a while, my curiosity got the better of me and I decided to stroll through the cemetery. I was fascinated by the various Dutch names engraved on the tombstones. When I saw the name *Fientje* (Feenche), I decided to add to the mystery of my identity by taking that pleasant-sounding name as my own.

When Mr. DeJong arrived, I hurried to meet him. He was a pleasant-looking man in his late 50s or early 60s dressed in farmer's clothes with suspenders, plaid shirt and a cap. I recognized him at once from Mother's description. "Follow me quickly," he said as he led me down the road to his farm.

The farmhouse sat next to two barns with tulip fields across the road. I could smell the salty air from the sea which lay out of sight of the house, just over the sand dunes in the rear of the property. When we entered the farmhouse, the aroma made my mouth water. A short chubby woman with the most wonderful smile came out of the kitchen. Her hair was wound in a large, dark-brown braid perched on the top of her head. The DeJongs were Seventh-day Adventists and her plain, high-collared dress with the long sleeves and simple design was in the tradition of their religion.

"Welcome, child," she said as she wrapped her arms around me in a warm hug. "We're so glad the Lord brought you here." She took me quickly into the kitchen and gave me a glass of milk and a piece of warm bread. I knew I would be safe with this woman.

As I ate, Mrs. DeJong asked me about my trip. Then she explained that I was to tell people I was her niece from the big city who was staying with their family for awhile because food was scarce in the city due to rationing. "We must be very careful not to raise anyone's suspicions, Felie," she warned. "Even our neighbors cannot be trusted!"

I assured her I would be very careful. "Please call me *Fientje*," I said. "It's a pretty name and it will help me to remember that I am no longer Felie."

The DeJongs thought that was a good idea. Then they showed me to my bedroom and advised that I get to bed early as the family would be up and moving before daybreak to start their chores. Since I was going to be part of the family, tomorrow morning I would be expected to be up and moving, too.

Fientje, Fientje, I repeated over and over to myself as I settled under a down comforter. *Fientje from the big city.* Even though the name rolled off my tongue smoothly and the welcome had been warm, I cried myself to sleep that night and for many others as I thought of my mother, my home, and my family.

Chapter 5

In the morning, I woke with the smell of oatmeal wafting up the stairs. *I could lie here forever!* I thought as I snuggled even further into the warm bed. But soon curiosity got the better of me and I jumped out of bed, dressed and went down to see what was going on in the kitchen.

Mrs. DeJong's perky hello was like the sun shining into my heart. Her wonderful cooking warmed my stomach before I was sent out to the barn to see if I could help. Mr. DeJong welcomed me and told me to just look around and keep my eyes open. Once I learned what the workers were doing, he would let me help. So that day I watched as the workers sorted tulip bulbs into big strainers by size and color. After the bulbs were sorted, they were dried on screen–like flats in the attic of the barn. Their pungent, sweet odor filled the air. Although I was shy, the workers made me feel welcome. As a relative from the big city whose name was Fientje, my new life had begun.

Being busy during the day was a pleasant change as I had had quite enough of the boring and monotonous months spent in hiding in the attic in Amsterdam. I could hear the German trucks rumbling up and down the shoreline that lay beyond the fields behind the house. Mr. DeJong told me that the Germans were placing mines and building bunkers in the sand dunes all along the coast. We seldom saw soldiers in town except for those who manned the checkpoint between DeZilk and Hillegom. I was able to move about with relative freedom, but the soldier's presence just out of sight of the farmhouse was still intimidating. In the evenings I listened to German music blaring from the soldiers' radios while I worked on the study material and homework assignments that Mr. DeJong's son-in-law brought me. Early evening was the most lonely time for me as thoughts of Mother and concern for her and my grandparents seemed to always arrive after the supper dishes were washed and put away. Although studying helped me get through those dark hours before bed, the German music was a constant reminder of the reason for my sorrow.

After about five weeks, Mr. DeJong asked if I would like to visit my mother. Wow! Did he really have to ask? That night I was in bed earlier than usual, and up again the next morning ready to go without feeling like my head had even touched the pillow.

Mrs. DeJong filled a brown paper bag with fresh fruit and other items from the farm for me to take to her son and his family in Amsterdam. Then Mr. DeJong walked me to the bus stop in front of the church and I retraced my bus and train ride back to Mother. Finally I was at the young DeJong's apartment and in my mother's arms. It was a short hug, but long enough for me to feel how large she had grown in the few weeks I had been gone. She laughed when I placed my head against her belly to listen to the sounds of the growing baby. I was delighted!

The apartment was cramped to say the least; and, once again we had to remain quiet when the family left for work or went out. Even though I was only there for a day, I felt smothered. The time flew by and much too soon I had to begin my journey back to DeZilk. I dreaded leaving my loved ones behind, but in all honesty I looked forward to getting back to the freedom of the farm. The trip back would have been unbearable for me if I had known this was to be my last visit with Mother and Uncle Siegmund in Amsterdam.

Returning to DeZilk brought relief. I could leave the house, help in the barn, work around the yard, and do my schoolwork without restraint. But being in the country also brought isolation. In those days, the public was not allowed to use the telephone, so no one would be able to call me when the baby arrived. The Germans also prohibited the use of radios and often made random house calls to search for them along with anything else they might have the whim to inspect. Fortunately, in the country, they were much less likely to make such searches, but the people in the cities were subject to search at any time.

Early in June of 1943 I suddenly was faced with a personal problem. My body was going through changes I didn't understand. I was embarrassed and wanted my mother, but I had to go to Mrs. DeJong instead. She explained that I was becoming a young lady and God was preparing my body for motherhood. Then she gave me pads made from old sheets sewn together.

"Wash these and reuse them every month," she told me. "You'll be fine. Every woman bleeds every month from an egg that doesn't become a baby." This didn't make much sense to me, but Mrs. DeJong was too shy to tell me more so she told me Mother would explain everything to me later.

The DeJongs were Seventh-day Adventists and very religious. Saturday was their day of worship and prayer, the same day of worship my family had observed in our Jewish tradition. It had been a long time since I had had prayer time, so I looked forward to sitting in the family room listening to the DeJong's pray. It was also nice to bow my head and feel gratitude before each meal when the family held hands around the table and said grace.

When the DeJong's daughter visited, the adults would have a Bible study. I learned much during this time and found the Bible to be an interesting and exciting book from which to read and learn. The family spent many hours discussing biblical characters and their stories, many of which related to the difficult times we were going through.

Mr. DeJong strongly believed that God created everyone equal and that the light or dark color of your skin was for a special reason. "In some tropical climates, God created men darker to protect them from the heat," he told me one day. "Part of the Netherlands is the Dutch East Indies, so the native people there are always dark, Fientje. But always remember, they are still Dutch people. Don't ever forget, we are all God's children. He has created us all." This lesson has stayed with me and I am still extremely upset when I hear or see any form of racial prejudice.

One Monday morning in late June, just after breakfast, there was a frantic knock on the front door. Mrs. DeJong went to answer and Mother rushed in almost before the door opened.

Mrs. DeJong wrapped her arms around the shaking woman. Then she helped her off with her threadbare coat and settled her before the fire with a hot cup of tea. I went to get Mr. DeJong from the barn. After she calmed down a little, Mother told us the story.

"The Gestapo broke into the apartment and arrested Siegmund and Max," she gasped out between ragged breaths. "I happened to be standing with my coat on because the room was so cold. I was holding my black pocketbook that I keep with me at all times because it holds all my important papers. It looks like a doctor's bag. So, when the Gestapo arrived, I pretended I was a nurse with a sick patient waiting for me. They told me to go; but, instead of going downstairs where I knew there would be other agents outside the apartment who might not be as easily fooled, I hurried up the stairs to the roof. Several of the townhouses are attached to one another in a row, so I climbed out onto our roof and slithered across the adjoining roofs to the last house where I hid and waited to see what would happen. Then, later, I rushed down the stairs to the back street and forced myself to stroll to the train station so I wouldn't arouse suspicion. I bought a ticket for Haarlem and once I got there, I caught the bus to DeZilk."

As Mother caught her breath, I cried out, "But where's the baby? What did you have? Do I have a brother or a sister? Where is it?"

"Shush, Felie," Mother scolded. "I'll tell you about that later. Sit down over there while I talk to the DeJongs."

I slumped down on the floor and listened as the DeJongs asked about their son and his wife.

"The Gestapo dragged them to the street corner," Mother told them. "They shot them with their hands tied together in front of the neighbors who were forced from their homes and made to watch. Then they announced that the same thing would happen to anyone else harboring Jews in their homes. They threw Max and Siegmund into a truck and left."

Mr. DeJong held his wife as they wept and prayed together. Their pain was increased because they couldn't claim the bodies of their loved ones. Inquiries would draw Gestapo attention to them and expose us to capture. We thought that under the circumstances they would no longer let us stay with them, but these dear people had a remarkably strong faith and sense of justice. They believed without a shadow of a doubt that their son and daughter-in-law were in heaven and God had sent Mother and me to them for safekeeping. From his prayer we could tell that Mr. DeJong was even more determined than ever to help us survive the war.

I couldn't wait one second longer! "Mother," I demanded, "what about the baby?"

"Your baby sister was born on June 6," she told me, "and I named her Suzi. I had her in the attic of Dr. Guckal's apartment. I had a real hard time because I'm so small. Dr. Guckal stuffed a handkerchief in my mouth to keep me from screaming out loud. I still have a bad cough because of that."

"So where's the baby?"

"After she was born, I gave her to Dr. Guckal. She had made arrangements with a Gentile woman who was brave enough to fool her neighbors into believing she was pregnant. She wore a pillow under her skirt for several months and told everyone the pregnancy was an accident. She already has two grown daughters, but she and Dr. Guckal planned the whole thing before our Suzi was born just in case she had a chance to save a Jewish newborn."

"But Mother," I wailed. "She's our baby. When can we get her back! and how will we prove she's ours if the woman wants to keep her?"

"Don't worry, Felie," she assured me. "Before I gave her to Dr. Guckal I covered her mouth so no one would hear her screams and we held her tiny left foot on a hot water bottle. The burn from the hot metal was deep and surely will have left a permanent scar that will help me identify Suzi. Only Dr. Guckal and I know about this. So, when I go back for Suzi, I'll have proof she is mine."

Well, the plan didn't sound too good to me, but I didn't say so as the adults were already moving Mother upstairs to my bedroom. Once there, she fell into a deep sleep.

From that day on, Mr. DeJong put all his efforts into resisting the Germans. He worked for the underground in many ways he never talked about. But we knew when he left the house at night instead of going to bed as usual that he was meeting with others in the Dutch Resistance.

It was exciting when he brought home crystal components and hooked up a receiving set in the basement so he could hear news of the war. It was even more exciting when the English used gliders to parachute information leaflets and sacks of materials into the fields near us.

Sometimes Mr. DeJong would take me with him and we would walk through the fields at dusk shining flashlights around as we searched the area for the dropped materials. If anyone questioned what we were doing, we could say we were merely taking our evening walk before bedtime. As soon as we located a parachute we would bury it along with the items attached to it. After a few days, Mr. DeJong would go to the fields in the early morning hours and retrieve the material. He would cut portions off the parachute and bring the strips home a few at a time. Then Mrs. DeJong would sew things from the pieces of silk.

One evening, Mr. DeJong smuggled in a small printing press and soon he began to print an underground newspaper with information dropped in from England, along with what he received from his underground contacts. One day he asked me to go into Hillegom, a small town about seven kilometers away, to deliver these newspapers. "You can hide them inside this large baby carriage beneath a blanket," he told me. "Anyone who sees you will think you're taking your doll for a walk."

This sounded like quite an adventure to an eleven year old, so I loaded up the carriage and became a resistance fighter. I sang as I pushed my carriage along the road. When I approached the German checkpoint, my heart was in my throat. But the soldiers were so busy playing cards they didn't even glance at me as I strolled by.

My instructions were to go to an address in Hillegom, ring the bell and ask for the dentist. The address was located in a row of old, attached houses made of stone. Each house had a small garden in the front. "Most of the houses look the same," Mr. DeJong told me, "so be very careful that you go to the right one."

I found the house number, checked it again and then rang the bell. A man's voice came from the back of a room that was pitch black to me because I had just come out of the sunlight.

"What do you want?" the voice grumbled.

"Do you like my doll?" I answered as I had been instructed to.

"Leave the doll," the dentist said. "Park the carriage inside the entrance and leave."

I parked the carriage with the hidden newspapers inside the entrance and went outside. A few minutes later, the empty carriage was shoved out the door to me.

The walk back home was long, but I never tired. I enjoyed the exercise, and the now-empty carriage was lighter so I was able to play the game of avoiding stepping on the cracks in the pavement to pass the time. The adults were relieved when they spotted me coming down the road and Mr. DeJong rushed out to meet me. He seemed especially pleased when I told him, "the guards never even looked up when I went by." I became the official courier and the trip was repeated every few days as Mr. DeJong and his printing press worked during the nighttime hours to spread news and helpful information to the Dutch citizens.

The best part of each trip for me was when I arrived home and was met by the wonderful aromas coming from Mrs. DeJong's living room. She would be at the warm wood stove preparing the evening meal. Since the DeJongs were vegetarians, we often had stew made from the vegetables grown in the family garden. I didn't mind the meals, but Mother missed the meat and fish she was accustomed to.

As much as I loved her, it was hard for me to have Mother living with us. She was so deeply depressed that she would sit around in a cloud of gloom most of the day. At night I would go to sleep with her muffled sobbing in my ears. I tried to cheer her up by telling her about all that we would do when the war was over. Sometimes this would work and she would begin to feel better. But most of the time she talked about her parents, her brother and her sisters—especially Aunt Ida.

Before the war, Aunt Ida had been making plans to travel to America to live with our third cousin, Esther. But, before she could leave, Ida fell in love and decided to stay in Holland and get married. So, Sabina, her younger sister, traveled to America in her place. Sabina married a wonderful man named Albert and the couple raised two lovely daughters.

Although Ida eventually broke her engagement, she never did make it to America. She remained in Holland with Oma and Opa. After the war we learned that in order to keep from being sent to a work camp she had volunteered to accompany a train full of Jewish children who were being deported to Germany. She had no idea that these poor children were being wrenched from their parents' arms just before the parents were herded into cattle cars for their trip to the concentration camps. Little did Aunt Ida know that she and the children she so lovingly wanted to help were being transported to Buchenwald where the whole trainload of them were gassed to death without even leaving the railroad cars they were traveling in.

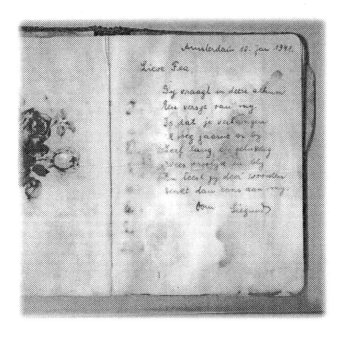

Dear Faye,
    You asked me in this album
    A verse from me,
    If that is your request,
    I will gladly add to it.
    "Live long and happy,
    Be glad and cheerful,
    And when you read these words
    Then think of me.

        – Uncle Siegmund

Chapter Six

Mother's depression lifted a little when an English flyer came to stay with us. We learned later that he was an intelligence agent who parachuted in to work with the underground. At the time, we thought he was a friend of the DeJong's who had come to visit for a while. In my mind, James was a gift from God because he spent a lot of time with Mother and she thrived on his attention. It must have been wonderful for her to have a friend her own age who understood her situation. They spent many evenings before the fire playing games and talking. James held out the hope that the war would soon be over. After a while, I realized that he and Mother had become more than friends and I was happy for her. I liked him a lot and the affection the two shared lifted Mother's gloom which made my life easier.

Mother never felt safe enough to leave the house. I, on the other hand, went about freely and sometimes even ventured beyond the farm. However, I couldn't go too far because we never knew when the German soldiers camped in the sand dunes would decide to come into town. Their closeness made Mother extremely nervous, so Mr. & Mrs. DeJong made a hiding place under the floor board in their bedroom closet beneath the spot where they normally kept their shoes. The hiding place was covered by a carpet. Mother and I planned to use this hiding place if the Germans ever came to the farmhouse.

One morning a fist rapped against the front door. Mrs. DeJong motioned for us to go upstairs. We had no time to get into the bedroom closet to hide before we heard loud voices in the living room. "Where are your bicycles, batteries or radios?" one soldier asked. "And where are the rest of the people who are living here?" said another.

Mother didn't wait to hear any more. She rushed me to our room and sat me on a bed pan with my clothes on. Then she stuck a thermometer in my mouth and draped a blanket over my shoulders.

Heavy boots tromped up the stairs and there was a loud knock on our door. A young German soldier walked in. "Verzeihung!" he said when he saw me sitting on the bed pan. "Excuse me!" I had to bite my cheeks to keep from giggling at the sight of his beet-red face as he rushed from the room. Mother chuckled in relief as we listened to his boots stumbling down the steps.

But when the soldiers left and Mother went looking for James her chuckles turned to sobs of despair. "He escaped and is hiding in the woods," Mr. DeJong told her. "I'm not sure it will be safe for him to come back here. The troopers asked us where the man was who was visiting us. I told them the only man we knew of had come from the city looking for food and he left when we told him we had nothing for sale." At that report we both were sure we would never see or hear from James again.

Things were getting noisy around DeZilk. The British were bombing the railroad tracks near our farmhouse during the night, so the Germans spent their days repairing the tracks. Rail lines were important to them because they used them to transport men and supplies around as well as to move the confiscated Jewish-owned valuables back to Germany. The same pattern repeated itself day after day, night after night: the Germans transporting valuables in the daytime, the British bombing the railroad tracks at night. I often watched this activity from our bedroom window. When the bombs fell too close, we would leave the house and lie flat in the tulip field behind the barn.

Unfortunately, the nightly bombing raids and the shortage of gasoline for the bus stopped Mr. DeJong's monthly trips to Amsterdam. He no longer could get our support money from Uncle Siegmund's secretary. The export sales of tulips in the spring and tobacco in the fall had stopped with the war so the DeJong's were forced to rent out their dining room and their daughter's empty bedroom upstairs to bring in some much-needed cash.

A young couple in the area were getting married just at that time and were looking for a place to rent. So, right after their wedding day, they moved in with us at the farm. Mr. DeJong made a partition in the dining room so we could go into the kitchen for water and food without disturbing the newlyweds. He also put a small, pot-bellied stove in front of the fireplace on their side of the dining room so they could heat their room and cook their meals on it.

Mother became good friends with the young couple, and they often played cards together to pass away the time. Since the DeJongs' religious doctrines didn't allow them to use tobacco or play cards, they didn't join in. They were older and their interests were quite different from the younger adults who shared their home. The time their tenants spent at their games allowed the DeJongs to enjoy some of the privacy they had given up to help us all out.

Not too long after they came to stay with us, Donna announced she was pregnant. I couldn't wait for the baby to arrive, but Mother was greatly saddened as she watched her new friend prepare for her first child. Our circumstances made it impossible for Mother to tell of her joy at the birth of her own baby or share her pain and loss.

Although it must have seemed like a long nine months to Donna, they flew by for me until the morning when I woke up and heard a lot of bustling about in the kitchen. I went downstairs to see what was going on and found Mr. DeJong pumping water and heating it on the stove in the DeJongs' living room. "The baby's coming," Mother told me as she and Mrs. DeJong bustled back and forth with bowls of water and dry towels. Mr. DeJong winced every time Donna shrieked in pain. After a particularly loud cry, there was a moment of silence and then a tiny voice wailed a hello to the world.

"It's a healthy boy," Mrs. DeJong announced as she poked her head into the kitchen. What a thrill! The happy event picked up Mother's spirits and lifted the dullness from our routine days. She and Mrs. DeJong spent hours hand sewing baby clothes from old bed linens, and diapers and towels from old sheets. The arrival of this new life brought renewed hope to all of us and we were once again aware of God's love even in this time of man–made darkness.

The family stayed with us for about a year. Then they moved to a nearby farm where Donna's husband found work. As we waved goobye I knew their going would leave an empty place in our home and hearts.

While Mother spent her days in the house, I preferred to be outside as much as possible. I often helped in the barn tending to the tobacco leaves that the DeJong farm grew. We would cut the big veins of the leaves open and then wrap them in bundles. Normally, the bundles would hang from the ceiling only until they were completely dried, but now they remained hanging waiting for the war to end so they could once again be exported.

After a full day of such work, we were hungry, but there was seldom enough food to go around even though we grew our own vegetables. Since sugar was scarce, Mrs. DeJong would boil beets until they became syrupy and then dab that concoction onto our food to sweeten it. She also barbecued tulip bulbs until they were deep brown and then roasted them and ground them into a coffee substitute. After perking, the taste was vile! Even today I detest coffee, the best blends taste like ground tulip bulbs to me.

The winter of 1943–44 was long and cold. We sat around with nothing to do until the boredom sank Mother even deeper into depression. I talked often about the war ending and finding my sister, but not even that would pick up Mother's spirits now.

To make matters worse, one of her teeth had developed an abscess and she was in great discomfort. The pain became too much to bear, so Mr. DeJong encouraged her to take a trip out of our semi-safe area to visit the dentist in Hillegom.

"I'm afraid my false papers won't clear inspections at the checkpoints," she told the DeJongs. "I'll just suffer until the pain goes away."

But after Mr. DeJong watched her walk the floors in agony with no relief in sight, he made underground arrangements with the dentist I had been delivering the newspapers to.

"Go in the early morning," Mr. DeJong advised. "The Germans will be half asleep or hung over from the liquor they drink every night. You should pass through easily. If you take Fientje with you, you'll be less conspicuous."

Mother's pain finally surpassed her fear. With a scarf covering her face so she would look like a farmer's wife, we began our trip. As we approached the checkpoint, my heart was pounding so hard I was certain the guards would hear, but they didn't even ask to check our papers. They must have been so used to seeing me walk by that they just watched as we passed right through their station and hurried on to the dentist's office.

The dentist was waiting for us and he quickly extracted Mother's tooth. When she tried to pay him, he shook his head. "No, no!" he said. "You need the money much more than I do." We were certain now that he knew we were Jews and he was happy to help us.

On the trip home, the guards were distracted by a farmer with a cart full of hay so we again passed the checkpoint without being asked for our papers. Mother and I didn't speak to each other as we walked. We both were tired and emotionally drained by the stress. So, when we came to the small white church in DeZilk, I was surprised when she said, "Let's stop here for a minute, Fientje." She peeked in and when she found no one inside we went in and sat in a seat for a while. The rest soon renewed us. As we left, I thanked God for being with us on this trip.

When Spring arrived everyone was anxious to get outdoors. The fresh air was so exhilarating that I went out as much as possible to breathe it in. I even looked forward to helping with the farm chores and was disappointed on my first morning out when the farm hands told me there wasn't much I could do to help. So I went back inside to help Mrs. DeJong with breakfast. As we worked, Mrs. DeJong mentioned that she would love to eat something different for a change. "A nice warm piece of bread with jelly would sure taste good," she said. Although the bakery was still open, bread was a luxury in our household now. With so many mouths to feed, Mrs. DeJong had been stretching her rationing coupons by buying oats and rice instead of more expensive things like bread. The menu had been porridge for breakfast and rice for lunch for most of the winter.

"Boy, me too!" I agreed. "I can't wait until this war is over so I can have a piece of Oma's angel food cake covered with cherry sauce."

After we washed the dishes and went to our room to make the beds for the day, Mother said, "Here Fientje. Take this money and go to the bakery we passed on our trip to the dentist. Ask the baker if you can buy some bread without using food coupons or rationing stamps. But don't tell Mrs. DeJong where you're going. We'll try to surprise her."

I wasn't surprised that Mother had money. She was a woman who always had a "knipple"—a spare dollar hidden anywhere and everywhere. In fact, in our family, she had the reputation of being someone who was always able to find an extra coin or two when needed. So, after listening to a long list of instructions on what to do and how to be careful and how I should hurry back, I set out on my journey.

The trip went well and I skipped along until I got close to the bakery where I stopped to watch a group of children who were playing a version of jump rope called *double Dutch*. I was delighted when one of the girls asked if I wanted to play. What a silly question! They were asking a girl who had been cooped up with adults for what seemed like an eternity. I jumped right in and soon was laughing and having a great time.

After a much–too–short time, Mother's words "come back quickly, Fientje" popped into my head. "I'm sorry. I must leave," I told my new friends. "I have to get home to help prepare supper."

"What are you having?" the youngest girl asked,

"We're making *Heete Bliksen,*" I told her. "It's a dish of apples, potatoes, and nutmeg mashed into a stew."

"Do you have any bread to go with it?" her older sister asked.

"Oh, no," I answered. "We haven't had any bread for a long time."

"Wait a minute," she said as she opened the door and went into the bakery. In a few minutes she came back with a large loaf of fresh brown bread and handed it to me. The smell literally made my mouth water. When I took out my coins to pay for it, she waved me away.

"We don't want your money," she said. "Take the bread home to your family. My father owns the bakery."

I was a proud and happy girl in the center of attention that Sabbath evening when Mrs. DeJong placed the bread at the head of the table and told everyone they could thank me for it. Then she added to the surprise by bringing out a jar of strawberry jam she had preserved and saved for a special occasion. With great delight we spread the crimson treat over the fresh bread and complete silence fell as we savored every bite.

The camaraderie and good spirits on such occasions helped us to survive the war. We had no electricity, telephone, running water or indoor plumbing. Our bathroom was a water closet with a hole beneath a seat. We used old catalogues for toilet paper and always finished by pumping water from a hand-pumped well in the kitchen into a bucket and carrying it back to the water closet so that the next person would have it ready for use.

Our kitchen had a stone sink, a wood burning oven, a hand pump located over the sink, and a wood-block table in the middle on which we cut our vegetables. The family ate no meat or fish, and they only ate eggs if the chickens in our barn laid them. We traded fruits and vegetables with the neighbors to add some variety to our diets. Many of these foods the family would store in the cool basement of their traditional Dutch farmhouse for the winter.

The gift of bread made that Sabbath special for me, but every Sabbath was special for the DeJongs. It began at sunset on Friday. Up until then, Mrs. DeJong spent the day dusting the living room from top to bottom. She aired the rest of the house out while Mr. DeJong cleaned the ashes from the pot-bellied stove that stood in the middle of the living room. Everything smelled so clean and fresh.

On Friday evening, before Sabbath began, we took our weekly baths. Mrs. DeJong boiled water on the wood stove and filled a round metal tub that Mr. DeJong brought into the living room and set next to the fireplace. Did that bath feel good! After soaking and scrubbing, we put on clean clothes and then slept in them because it was too cold to change from daytime clothes into nightdresses for sleep.

Mrs. DeJong's weekly pattern of chores was followed religiously. On Monday, washday, she took out a large tub and filled it with water pumped by hand from the well. Then she scrubbed each item on a washboard. Every piece was put through a hand-cranked ringer, into a rinse tub and then cranked through the ringer again. The clothes were hung in front of the pot-bellied stove to dry.

Tuesday was the day for ironing and mending. On Wednesday, everyone cleaned the upstairs bedrooms. Thursday was the day to prepare and cook the beans and other vegetables that would be used for the Sabbath and weekend meals. Friday was the day for final cooking, cleaning of the living room and family bath time. Finally, Saturday arrived—a sacred day filled with Bible study and prayer. The DeJongs' daughter, son-in-law, and their children would join us and we would sing hymns and pray together. They would also stay for the noon meal.

On Sunday I would go to the Catholic church so it would appear to any Germans watching that I belonged in town. I had learned to make the sign of the cross before I entered the pew and then to kneel to pray before sitting back in the seat. The best part of the service for me was the glances I stole at the young man sitting across the aisle.

After I returned from church, we would eat and then spend the afternoon reading or playing board games in order to keep our part of the neighborhood quiet in respect for those who honored God on Sunday instead of Saturday like we did. This day–by–day routine carried on from week to week as long as I was with the family and it provided me with a comforting sense of stability.

As the days passed into months and months into years, I began to notice changes in my body that embarrased me. My rounding figure was attracting stares from some of the farm boys and I found myself blushing quite often. Here, in mid–1944, at twelve–and–a–half, I was rapidly becoming a woman. The change took me by surprise.

I found myself spending more of my time hanging out at the milking farm just down the road. I told Mother I was hoping to get some free milk for the family, but the more truthful reason was that the boy I had been looking at in church on Sunday was in the barn at milking time. One day, I asked if he needed some help.

"Sure," he said. "Sit down and I'll show you how to milk a cow."

I tried and tried, but I just couldn't seem to get the hang of it. Only after Jaap demonstrated the technique several times was I able to produce a white stream and hit the pail with it. After his chores were finished, Jaap gave

me a liter of milk to take home. I had had a great day! I
finally had made a friend of this tall, blond-haired,
blue-eyed Dutch boy and as a bonus I pleased the
DeJongs with my contribution to the evening meal. Mrs.
DeJong made some of the milk into a dessert that tasted
like yogurt. And, to make it a really special treat, she
added fresh fruit.

Mother, on the other hand, hadn't had a good day.
She didn't even want to listen when I tried to tell her
about Jaap. But then none of Mother's days were good.
Her ever-deepening depression kept her behind a wall of
tortured emotions. If I asked her a question about boy/girl
matters, she would never say enough to help me. And I
had so many questions! In my innocence, I thought if you
kissed a boy you would have a baby. I could sense Jaap
looking at me like he was thinking of kissing me and I
knew if we were alone in the barn it wouldn't take him
long to try. What should I do about that?

I was scared but also flattered that Jaap showed this
interest. These confused feelings plagued me. Of course,
they didn't bother me enough to keep me from going back
to the barn as often as I could. Many other farm children
hung around like I did looking for handouts of milk or
butter, but I was older than most of them and closer to
Jaap's age.

After a while I became quite good at milking, and
one day Jaap asked if I would go for a walk with him
after the chores were done that evening. My heart melted
as I looked into his blue eyes. I was dying to accept his
invitation, but I was too afraid of my feelings and of the
Germans who were hunkered down in bunkers in the sand
dunes between the farms and the North Sea. I couldn't
tell Jaap I was a Jew who was afraid of the Germans, so
I told him the DeJongs' wouldn't let me go out walking
with a boy. That ended my budding romance—and the

free milk. The next day, when I arrived at the farm, Jaap wouldn't look at me. I had hurt his feelings, but, even though it broke my heart to lose his friendship, I couldn't tell him who I really was. No one could be trusted!

The Catholic Church of De Zilk, where I first saw Jaap. I worshipped there on Sundays as part of my disguise

Chapter Seven

On June 6, 1944, my baby sister's first birthday, we received the hopeful report of the invasion in France. The German soldiers located in the dunes behind the farm must have found the report frightening because not long after we heard the news we began to hear the growl of motors as they started to move heavy equipment and vehicles. Mr. DeJong became less cautious now and listened to the radio reports during the daytime as well as at night. We waited in tense anticipation for the latest developments and tracked each advancement of the soldiers in the invasion force.

As fall and winter dragged into spring, the Allied advances slowed and we sat in our farmhouse world waiting and waiting. During the winter the Nazis had cut off food shipments by rail to towns and cities throughout Holland. The lack of food brought thousands of women and children from Amsterdam and other cities and towns to the country looking for food. During these *hongertochts*—hunger walks—people with baby carriages and pushcarts trudged for hours in freezing weather to reach a farm. They often searched for a week or more just to find some flour, a few potatoes and carrots or kale. They would bring valuables with them to trade for the produce. Those who could not get enough food lined up at public kitchens in the cities for free gaarkenken, a soup broth made of sugar beets, potatoes or carrots. We learned later that at their peak, Amsterdam's public kitchens had served 300,000 people. Although the Swiss and Swedish Red Cross sent food, the Dutch people only were able to get about 500 calories a day. Many stayed alive by eating tulip bulbs. Most of the 140,000 Jews who lived in Holland had been deported and sent to Mauthausen, Auschwitz, Theresienstadt, and Bergen-Belsen. Before the war ended 110,000 of these Dutch Jews were dead. If Mother and I had known of this, our fear would have been much worse.

On a clear, quiet night in March of '45, we were sitting in the family room when we heard a soft knock on the back door. Mother and I raced upstairs to hide as Mr. DeJong went to see who was there. We were pretty sure it wasn't anyone to worry about since the Germans usually stormed through the front door with much shouting and pounding.

Our sensitized ears picked up the sound of soft whispering from the kitchen and then light footsteps on the stairs. "It's all right," Mr. DeJong called as he opened the bedroom door. "Come and see what a surprise I have for you."

We opened the door to the closet and looked out. Mother gave a cry of joy and rushed to embrace James, the friend we had thought was lost to us forever. "I parachuted down behind the barn," he told us. "I've been sent back to work with the underground. Boy, am I glad to see you two are still here!"

We gathered around the stove and listened for hours as James explained that he was an intelligence agent, something only Mr. DeJong had known before. Then he spoke about the invasion and the Allied forces and their plans. "Germany's defeat is a sure thing," he assured us. "The German soldiers are cold and hungry and their morale is low. Some are even offering the Dutch resistance fighters weapons and motorbikes in exchange for places to hide until the war is over."

We listened to James until we couldn't keep our eyes open any longer. But, before we went to bed, Mr. DeJong volunteered to go to the field to recover James' parachute. I was glad that James thought we should leave it alone for a few days so we wouldn't call attention to his arrival. I was much too tired for an evening stroll.

I can't seem to remember James' last name, but I do remember the taste and smell of the packs of chewing gum he brought me. I also remember how good his smile made me feel and how Mother's spirits soared as she spent hours talking with him by the stove.

On April 30 we heard that Adolf Hitler had committed suicide. Then, on May 4, the Germans surrendered unconditionally to Allied Field Marshal Bernard Montgomery. On May 5, 1945, Mr. DeJong had been in the basement for hours listening to his short wave radio. He suddenly bellowed, "The Germans have surrendered. The Germans have surrendered!" No one moved or said a word. We just didn't believe it was true. Then Mrs. DeJong looked out the window and began to weep. The neighboring farm families were hugging each other and dancing in the street. Suddenly the churchbells began to ring and we ran outside to join in the celebration.

Even after a day and night of rejoicing we still seemed incapable of believing this was true. Only when we saw the young German soldiers leave their bunkers and march by our house did it seem real. Most of the soldiers were young—perhaps sixteen or seventeen years old—and many were crying. As they marched by, some of our neighbors spat at them in hatred. Since the DeJongs were too Christian to spit, I didn't either; but, unlike them, I did dance and shout. It was the first time in a very long while that I saw a true smile on my mother's face. Our war was over!

A few days of partying went by before Mother began to talk about going home to Amsterdam. She and James spent hours with Mr. DeJong discussing our route and transportation needs. Since the trains and buses weren't running and the Germans had taken our bicycles along with everything else that had wheels, Mother and I were stuck with no way to get to Amsterdam except for a long and dangerous walk.

"Don't worry, Fientje," James assured me. "I'll get you two back to Amsterdam somehow."

Each night I would pray that God would help James find something for us to travel on. Then I would lull Mother to sleep with stories of how we would soon be back in our beloved city with our dear little Suzi.

After much discussion, Mother and Mr. DeJong finally decided the safest route would be the same one the bus traveled from Amsterdam to DeZilk. As each step of the return was planned out, my stories at night became more vivid. "We'll move right back into our apartment, Mother," I would whisper. "Oma and Opa will come out of hiding and so will Uncle Paul and his family. Aunt Ida will come home and we'll all be together when we find Suzi and bring her home to meet the family."

Boy, was I naive! We hadn't heard about the concentration camps at Buchenwald, Bergen–Beltzen and Auschwitz. The lack of communication with the rest of the world had sheltered us from the harsh realities of life in other parts of Holland. The radio reports we received had told only of the progress of the battles and the invasion of the Allies. We had no idea that all of our family and friends were lost to us forever. But our ignorance was a blessing because Mother's depression was deep enough with the situation as we knew it. I don't think she would have endured if she realized what we would be facing at the end of the war.

Days went by as I reveled in my daydreams. Then one afternoon James came in the back door carrying a large box and wearing a huge grin.

"Open it up," he told us. We did, and to our delight found the parts for two bicycles. "I just couldn't find the tires anywhere," he said.

"Don't worry a bit," Mr. DeJong said. "I'll assemble the bikes and make the wheels out of thin strips of fir." Two happy ladies embarrassed him as they jumped up and smothered him with hugs and kisses. James laughed so hard he choked. I ran and got him a glass of water. After the commotion stopped, I noticed there were only two seats in the box.

"There's only two seats, James. Where's yours?" I asked.

"I can't go with you, Fientje," he answered. "I have to stay in DeZilk to disarm any mines or bombs the Germans left in the sand dunes. The people are curious and they are going to see what the Germans may have left in the bunkers. It's dangerous because they don't know that the things that are hidden can hurt them. When I get that job done, I'll be going home to England."

I was surprised to hear that James was not coming with us, but my disappointment was soon overtaken by the hustle and bustle in our previously peaceful neighborhood. The British planes were landing on the hour with food and personnel who came to see what the townspeople needed after the long siege.

Mrs. DeJong, Mother, and James spent evenings discussing what essentials we would be able to take on the trip to Amsterdam. Sentimental things and extras would not fit on the bicycles, and even though we had very few possessions, we still had to make some hard choices. Mother was not pleased when I stood my ground and refused to leave the doll that had made the trip to DeZilk with me on the train. She seemed like part of the family and I would have given up a warm shirt before I left her behind.

It seemed to me that everyone in town was hustling except for James and Mr. DeJong. I watched them every day when they were able to take time from their own work to assemble our bicycles. They took, what was to my impatient nature, a ridiculously long time. As he had promised, Mr. DeJong fashioned the tires from tree bark. I clapped in glee when he placed metal clips around the bark to keep it in place and the wheels made a loud clicking sound as the metal hit the surface of the road. It would be a noisy trip, but the sound was music to my ears. I couldn't wait to take my first ride.

On May 16, we awoke early. As I looked out my bedroom window for the last time, the sun was peeking over the horizon and promising a beautiful day for travel. The tulip fields were at the end of their blooming period and the air was fresh with spring flowers. Mrs. DeJong outdid herself with breakfast treats served with an extra pat on my head each time she walked by me. I was torn between leaving this wonderful family and getting on the way, but Mother had no such problem. "Let's get going, Felie," she said as she quickly thanked the DeJongs for their help. "We have a long way to go today." Then she gave James a quick hug and climbed on her bicycle.

I laughed out loud when she wobbled down the drive toward the street. She hadn't ridden a bicycle since she was a little girl and it showed. With wet eyes and a heart full of love, I gave Mrs. DeJong a last squeeze, climbed on my bicycle and followed Mother down the street toward what I hoped would be a smooth trip back to Amsterdam.

We rode side by side on a bicycle path toward Haarlem and stopped for the first time about 13 kilometers from DeZilk so Mother could rest. She assured me she was all right, but she looked exhausted. We ate some of the fruit Mrs. DeJong had packed for us, drank some water and then went on.

As we traveled toward the city, other bicycle riders passed us and I looked at them in surprise. They wore tattered clothing, were thin and haggard looking and their bicycle tires were home-made, too. I began to wonder just what we would find when we got to Amsterdam. We took another rest stop and sat on the grass at the side of road, then we continued on with sore backs and weakening legs.

When dusk settled in, I suggested we stop for the night but Mother insisted that we should continue. We had been traveling for about nine hours and I didn't think I could go much further. It was a miracle Mother had made it this far, but she kept going and I followed her until we finally saw the city skyline. That sight brought renewed energy to my strained legs and Mother also picked up her pace. We went to Oma and Opa's apartment, but no one answered the door. I was so disappointed! Mother didn't say a word. She just climbed back on her bicycle and rode off. I had to pedal hard to keep up with her.

It was beginning to get dark when we came to the street on which we had lived before we went into hiding. When we came to our old apartment complex, Mother literally fell off the bicycle. I helped her up and brushed off her shirt as she stood looking up at the building. We stood there for a long time before she finally climbed the steps and rang the bell. A man answered.

"My name is Rose Adam," she told him, "and this is my daughter Felie. We used to live here before the war and I have come for our belongings."

The man turned and called his wife to the door. When he told her what we wanted she said, "What belongings? When we rented this apartment, it was completely empty. I'm sorry for your problems, but we can't help you." Then, before Mother could say a word, the door slammed in her face.

Mother sank in a heap on the stairs. I didn't know what to do with her. We had brought no money with us as Mother had finally used up all she had. We couldn't go any further, so I knew I had to find a place where Mother could lie down and sleep before either of us could face our future.

"Come on, Mother, let's go to the park," I said with as much enthusiasm as I could muster. Princess Beatrix Park was only a couple of city blocks away; I had played there many times as a child. I hoped if I could get Mother away from the apartment complex she might feel better. So I helped her up and led her to our bicycles.

Her dazed eyes seemed to clear a little as she climbed back on the bicycle and followed me to the park. Was I surprised! I had thought we would be alone, but many other people were there with the same idea. Fortunately, it was a warm evening so we didn't have to worry too much about the late night and early-morning cold. When Mother and I found an empty bench we collapsed on it. Several young men who had been hiding out during the war lay on the grass nearby listening to a radio blasting the news of the day. The two of us couldn't help but listen as we huddled nearby.

"Come to the information and aid center for people returning home," a representative of the Red Cross urged. "We'll help you contact your family and friends."

"Let's go there tomorrow, Mother," I suggested. "You get some sleep now. Tomorrow everything will look better." After weeks of anticipation and hours of bicycling, we fell asleep in our beloved Amsterdam—home and free at last!

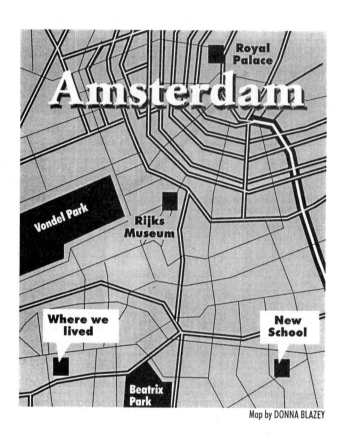

Map by DONNA BLAZEY

Chapter Eight

Daylight filtered through the leaves and we woke with empty stomachs and aching muscles. As I picked my stiff body off the bench and climbed aboard my bicycle it was hard for me to remember how wonderful it had looked when James and Mr. DeJong had finished assembling it. I don't know how Mother felt about hers, but mine suddenly looked and felt like a cruel monster.

We pedaled along listening to the tap, tap of the metal from our tires as we searched for the Red Cross Center. When we finally found it, we stood in a long line for hours before we were allowed into a room that reminded me of our school auditorium. Many blackboards were placed against the walls. A capital letter was at the top of each board. The boards encompassed the entire alphabet from *A* to *Z*. We were told to sign in with the worker who took care of the board with the first initial of our last name at the top. Luckily, with the name of *Adam*, I was near the top of the *A* board. I prayed I would find father's name or someone from his family listed there, too. On the other hand, Mother had been required by Dutch law to resume her maiden name of *Karafiol* after her divorce from father, so she signed in on the letter *K* board. A worker gave us a relief package of food and we devoured the contents on the spot. She also gave us a package of toiletries such as toothpaste, soap, washclothes, and other personal supplies. Then we joined another line to sign up for lodging.

The woman at the desk told us the lack of housing was critical. "Air raids, shellfire and street fighting have caused heavy damage," she said. "The Germans destroyed buildings during the Occupation and during the retreat they opened the dykes and sluices. Acres of land are flooded and will need to be drained before we can build or farm on them again. We have asked anyone with extra space in their homes to offer refugees temporary shelter until more permanent housing can be found. One such volunteer is Mrs. Brennan, an elderly woman who lives nearby. You can go there."

How fortunate we were to be placed with this wonderful woman who welcomed us into her home and became good friends with Mother. I snuggled into bed our first night there and fell asleep listening to the two women murmuring in the kitchen. My young spirit had kept me going—but now, after settling into this comfortable place, I felt quite ill. And Mother seemed worse off than I was. But, after a few days of Mrs. Brennan's wonderful care, we both were back on our feet and ready to begin again.

We spent time each day reading the blackboards at the Red Cross Center looking for our loved ones. The rest of the time, Mother searched for Dr. Guckal, the midwife who had helped her deliver and then hide my baby sister. She was the only one who knew which family had been taking care of Suzi and where they lived. Finding our baby took precedence over everything else.

One morning I asked Mother to take me to my friend Juliat's house so I could get the compass I had left with her. We walked back to our old neighborhood and rang the doorbell. "I wonder if she looks different," I whispered to Mother. "Won't she be surprised to see us!"

When Juliat opened the door, I recognized her immediately. She hadn't changed, she had just gotten bigger. "Hi, Juliat," I cried. "It's me, Felie. I've come to get my compass."

"I don't know what you're talking about," she said. "I don't know any Felie and I certainly don't have a compass." Then, without another word, she slammed the door in my face.

Mother gasped. I just stood on the step in stunned silence. Then we turned and walked to the Red Cross Center without saying another word. The betrayal of my friendship and trust caused a wound that never healed. After that I stopped searching for family. For days I could barely get myself dressed to sit at the window waiting for Mother to return from the Center. Each time she would return with the discouraging news. No family. No Suzi.

But one day, as I watched her come down the street I could see she was standing taller. When she came in, she was actually smiling. "I found Karafiol on the blackboard, Felie," she told me. "And the first initials are the same as Opa's and Oma's." That news got me up and going again. Early the next morning we rushed to the Center to see if we could get the address where the people were staying. After a long wait in another line, we finally got the information we were seeking. The people were my mother's second cousin and his wife, not my grandparents. I slumped down on the floor and wept.

"C'mon, Felie," Mother encouraged me. "It's a start. At least we have someone back who is family." It was unusual for me to be on the other end of such encouragement, so I picked myself off the floor and followed her. We left our address with the Red Cross worker so that when our cousin and his wife noticed Mother's name on the board, they could be told where we were living and that we were looking forward to seeing them.

One day we waited in line for coupons so we could get food and clothes that had been donated. What a wonderful feeling it was to have a full stomach and a change of clothes again. Finally something fit my newly-rounded body, and it made me feel quite grown up.

As the days went by and nobody else we knew signed in, we both became increasingly depressed. Mother would drag herself out of the house each day to look for a place for us to stay so we would have room for all of us when we found my sister. Finding her baby had become an obsession. Fortunately the kind people at the Red Cross Center were helpful and they were able to locate Dr. Guckal. She came to see us at Mrs. Brenner's and promised to take us to get the baby as soon as we found a place of our own. Then she offered to help us locate our new apartment.

On May 24, only a short eight days since we left DeZilk but what seemed an emotional lifetime, we found a small room in an apartment that an older couple was willing to share with us. They offered to close the dining room off from the living room to create a one-room apartment and we could share their kitchen and bath. PARADISE!

Amsterdam was without heat or electricity due to damage from the heavy bombing that took place during the last several weeks before the Germans surrendered. So once again we warmed ourselves in front of a pot-bellied stove that stood in the middle of the room. One large bed stood in one corner, and a table and four chairs in the other. The room was small but it was ours and all we needed!

The day after we moved in, Dr. Guckal arrived with a crib, a high chair, and a bath bowl. Mother was overcome. "Let's go get your daughter," the doctor said.

So we climbed into her small automobile with the M.D. license plate that allowed her to be one of the few in the city to get gasoline and left to get the baby we had been yearning for for so long.

"We will only visit with Suzi today," Dr. Guckal told us. "The people taking care of her think you should get to know her a little before you take her home with you. Tomorrow you can go back and get her for good."

My sister was a brown-eyed cutie with a head full of blond, bouncy curls that topped off a gigantic smile. When Mother knelt down and took her in her arms, it was like the two had never been apart. The woman who had been taking care of her made us feel welcome as did the family's two daughters who were about eighteen and twenty. It was obvious that they all loved our baby. Suzi had received good care and a lot of affection while she had been with them. It was evident in her trusting nature.

After an hour or so, we said goodbye. The family told us to return after Suzi's afternoon nap the next day. Mother and I agreed, but neither of us could sleep that night as we anticipated bringing our Suzi home.

At two the following afternoon, we set out to get her. When we arrived, she had just awakened from her nap. She gave us a big smile, and we couldn't wait to get her in the carriage to begin our trip home. Mother was gracious to the woman who had cared for her, but I just couldn't wait to get out of there. After many, goodbyes, thank yous and good wishes, we left these people and pushed our baby and her belongings home. She didn't have much, but what she had was just what we needed.

It was a joyful walk. As soon as we got into our apartment, Mother made some cereal only to find that our Suzi was a poor eater. She scrunched up her nose when we put the spoon in her mouth, rolled the cereal around, shoved it into her cheeks with her tongue so she looked like a chipmunk, then let some drip out of the corners of her mouth. Mother shoveled in some more and Suzi looked at her and did the same thing over again. She took about ten minutes to swallow one mouthful. No matter how Mother tried to coax her, Suzi wouldn't swallow what she obviously didn't like.

Giving our human doll her bath that first night was fun, and then Mother and I cuddled her and played with her until she couldn't stay awake a minute longer. It was the beginning of many days filled with Suzi's smiles, but Mother's heart was still heavy. She had learned from a posting at the Red Cross Center that her oldest brother Paul and his wife had found safe haven in Den Haag, but the wife's parents had not survived the camps. Mother had not received news of Oma, Opa, Aunt Ida or Aunt Toni. We learned later that Aunt Toni's daughter (the baby, Mother had given my clothes to) had been saved by some Belgian nuns.

Even though Paul and his wife had survived, he and Mother never reestablished their family ties. They had never gotten along for many reasons. Now she felt an even greater dislike for him because when he returned to Amsterdam he began to tell people "my sister and her two brats are in my pocket." This rumor that he was taking care of us financially infuriated Mother. He never gave her a dime! Now not only did she blame him for her parents' death, but also for tarnishing her reputation. She carried a grudge against him to her grave.

Mother continued her search for family and friends, but her greatest concern was to find a way to take care of her two young children. She needed a job.

Since she had been a more modern than traditional woman who had spent most of her life working not tending house, it seemed obvious that she should go into business for herself. She was good at fitting and designing ladies' clothes, but not much of a seamstress so she knew she needed someone who could sew while she fit and designed. A few years before the war, a Gentile woman had been hired to help with the mending at our house and at Opa's and Oma's. Now she searched this woman out and convinced her to become a partner in a new business they could run from our tiny apartment. I thought it was a great plan because Mother could take care of Suzi and me while still earning a living. Our small quarters would be difficult to work in, but we were on a waiting list for a larger apartment. Until that became available our one room would have to do.

To get the business off the ground and keep us going until some money began to come in, Mother contacted Uncle Siegmund's former secretary and asked her for more help. The woman refused. "The war is over now," she said. "I have no orders for any continued support for you."

Then, out of nowhere, a distant cousin of Siegmund's signed in at the Red Cross Center. Mother made contact with him and told him of the baby. He denied knowing Mother or ever hearing of a baby being born to his cousin. In reality, he and his wife had spent several Friday evenings at our old apartment eating dinner and visiting with Mother and Uncle Siegmund before we went into hiding. When he said he had never heard of his cousin's plans to marry Mother or that she was expecting Siegmund's child, Mother was shocked.

Siegmund's secretary said she was going to turn over Siegmund's funds to the distant cousin because he was the only blood relative as far as she was concerned, so Mother went to the Red Cross for legal help. The problem was that she had no papers confirming her divorce from my father. Marriages and divorces were registered in City Hall and then posted, but many of the downtown buildings had burned during the bombings and City Hall was one of them. Mother had no papers to prove she was divorced from Ernest Adam or that she had married Siegmund. She also didn't have a formal record of Suzi's birth that would have named Siegmund as the father. The Red Cross advised her to go to court anyway in an attempt to resolve the matter.

So, day after day Mother went to court. Dr. Guckal testified that she had been at the delivery and was sure this was the child because of the identifiable scar from the burn on Suzi's left heel. When Mother asked the foster parents to testify, they refused because their only dealings had been through Dr. Guckal and they didn't have any idea who the father of the child was. Mother held a grudge against them for the rest of her life. In fact, once when Suzi was around ten years old, the couple stopped her in the street, told her who they were and asked her to give their best to Mother. When Suzi told her about meeting them, Mother hollered, "Don't ever talk to those people again. They are horrible!" Mother was an opinionated and unforgiving woman, and her war experiences didn't soften her personality one bit. After months of fighting, she lost the court case and all Siegmund's funds were turned over to the deceitful cousin.

While all this turmoil was going on I had my little sister to myself most of the time, and at thirteen, I loved it! I would take Suzi to the park in her carriage every day after spending hours waiting in long lines at the neighborhood stores trying to get our share of the food that was being sent to Holland from the United States and England. Each day we would wait for the chance to buy a few potatoes, some spinach, and some carrots. When the people in line would ask if Suzi was my baby, I would swell with pride. After getting the vegetables home, I would cook them over a wood stove filled with sticks we had picked up on our outings in the park. When the meal was ready, I would strain some into baby food for Suzi who still hated every bite she was forced to take. Then I would put her down for her nap, and by then I was so tired I would do the same.

Even when she got older, Suzi was a picky eater. She always exchanged the lunches Mother packed for her with her school friends. Mother would put butter on the sandwiches; Suzi hated butter. Mother would pack an apple; Suzi hated apples. Mother insisted on serving buttermilk, Suzi despised buttermilk. The battles over food waged on with Mother insisting Suzi sit at the table until all was eaten and Suzi hiding food in her apron and then her closet until it petrified. When she was about twelve years old, Mother finally gave up and let her eat what she wanted to. The battle of wills was over!

In late August, Mother took me to a meeting with the principal of the Montessori school I had attended before the war. We brought with us the books I had used when I was hiding in the country. After the principal looked at the books and tested me he seemed surprised to find I had kept up with the other students and was ready to enter vocational school for the upcoming fall term. My heart soared when he told Mother I was mature for someone who had been through so much and if all went as planned I would finish my schooling in two years.

So, in September, I entered a vocational school where we learned dressmaking, pattern making, styling, and sewing from self-designed patterns to finished products. After successfully completing the program, the school promised to place me in a first-class ladies' specialty store where I would create designs for them to sell to their customers.

Chapter Nine

As months passed and everyone tried to get their lives back to normal, I found myself facing the reality that Father, Oma, Opa, and two of my aunts were never coming back. It was almost too much for me to bear. I also missed my father's parents and his sister and my two cousins who had all fled to Peru. The longing for family and friends at times would be so strong, I would go to my bed and sleep just to get away from the mental pain. Fortunately, Suzi's cute smile and playful nature helped to keep me from total despair.

It helped also when Mother and I went back to the building where my grandparents had lived and asked if we could look in the attic for the valuables Oma had hidden there. Unlike the people in our old apartment, these people graciously let us in and we found everything just as we had left it. The people were amazed at what we showed them. We carried some of the things back home with us that day and asked if we could return for the rest when we found an apartment. They agreed to let us leave our things in hiding until we could find a place large enough to hold them. What a spirit-booster that was!

Mother spent time each day now looking for a bigger apartment. She followed up on one program or another that might help returning refugees like us. After one of those trips she asked me if I could remember some of the furniture in our old home and in particular a painting that hung over our dining-room buffet.

"I sure can," I told her as I pictured myself sitting in

the dining room doing my homework at the table that stood beneath that painting.

Mother grabbed a pad and pencil. "Draw it," she ordered.

I did the best I could as I sketched a rough drawing of the oil painting of Norwegian fiords and snow-covered mountains. A waterway held a man fishing from a small boat. I reproduced, in childish form, every detail of that painting including the look of the rocks on the shoreline.

"You must come with me tomorrow," Mother said. "The government is trying to make restitution for some of the valuable items lost during the war. If we can prove or come close to proving that we owned such beautiful and expensive items, we will get some compensation for our loss."

The next day we appeared before the government committee carrying a bundle of good crystal, vases and sterling silverware with the K monogram. They could see that we had owned valuable household items. Then they asked me to draw the sketch of the oil painting again, and I was able to do it quickly. Mother told them the name of the artist, and, from my sketch and his name, they determined the value of the oil painting.

A week later, just about ten days before I was to start at my new school, we received the happy news that we had our new apartment. Even though we had to climb three flights of stairs to get to it, we were in heaven. It had two bedrooms, a dining room, a living room, bath and kitchen. You couldn't keep Mother still as she prepared to move. I tried to get her to rest, but she was much too excited.

Then more good news. We would be given furniture, dishes, utensils, linens and all the rest of the things we needed to set up housekeeping. To this day, I still don't know exactly how we got it all, but I remember being told it was "wiedergutmachung" which meant that our government was giving it to dispossessed people and the German government would be forced to reimburse the Dutch government for what was provided to us refugees.

We received everything quickly because my last name began with the letter *A* and Mother was listed as the widow of a man who had died in a concentration camp. Since Mother never talked about that with me, I don't know what camp Father died in. I was just grateful that our good fortune came quickly. We grieved for our loved ones but we also knew we had been granted the gift of life and it was up to us to make the most of it.

Mother advertised her fashion and alteration business in hopes that as life began to return to normal, women would be looking for someone to restore their old clothes for them. Mother had an eye for fashion and she could take an old dress, change the skirt around and make the top into a sleeveless blouse. Then she might add some new buttons or lace and the outfit would look brand new. Since there were as yet no new dresses in the stores, her business soon flourished. Satisfied customers recommended her to their friends and she became so successful that Molly worked all day on the sewing machine while Mother did the fittings. I made deliveries when I got home from school. Sometimes I would even get a tip from a satisfied customer.

During the work day, Mother and Molly would often discuss the war. During one of those discussions Molly let it slip that her husband, a Dutch citizen, had served with the NSB—the despised Dutch Nazi party. These Nazi sympathizers were known to treat Jews even more harshly than the German SS agents did. Mother felt betrayed and from that day the two women couldn't seem to agree on anything. Before long, Molly left and Mother was in a real bind. She needed a seamstress, fast!

Fortunately, she had become friendly with the baker's wife in DeZilk who was an accomplished seamstress. So, she called this woman on the newly-restored telephone service and told her of the new business and her need for help.

"I've got my hands full here," the baker's wife said. Her eighth child was only a few months old. "But, my older sister Annie is a magician with a sewing machine. She and Kees are getting married soon and they're looking for a place in the city. He's an automobile spray painter and there's a tremendous demand for his work now. I'll bet Annie would love to work for you."

"Have them come to stay with me until they find a place to live," Mother offered. "Annie can help me with the sewing,"

So, right after the wedding, Annie and Kees arrived. They helped Mother convert an unused attic room into a bedroom and Annie immediately set to work helping Mother in the business. I learned a lot of good sewing shortcuts from her that helped me in my classes at the trade school.

Although life had settled into a pleasurable routine, our longing for family cast a shadow over our happiness. I guess that's why we were tempted when my Aunt Sabina wrote from America asking Mother to join her in New York. Sabina planted a seed of hope in Mother's head when she assured her she could do the same type of work in America that she was doing in Holland. We discussed the move often, especially when Sabina kept up the barrage of mail urging, "Come, come!"

It sounded inviting to me. Sabina had two daughters, one about the same age as Suzi. We also had second and third cousins living in New York, and they soon joined Sabina in sending us letters of invitation and encouragement. We finally agreed it would be the thing for us to do. So, in the fall of 1946, we went to the consulate in Den Haag and applied for emigration papers.

In June of 1947, I graduated from school and was placed with a first-class fashion clothing store in Amsterdam working in the alterations department. I loved the work and enjoyed bringing money home to Mother. My life was finally running smoothly. Then one afternoon, I found a surprise visitor in our apartment. Cousin Joseph had arrived from New York to surprise us.

"I came to see how things are with you," he told me. "I promised Sabina and Albert to bring you all back with me."

When he found out my permission papers to emigrate had arrived but Mother's and Suzi's hadn't come yet, he took Mother to Den Haag to see if they could speed up the approval process. While we waited for the official response, we enjoyed many evenings listening to Joseph's stories about how wonderful life would be for us in America. It was good to feel like part of a family again.

When he could postpone his business affairs no longer, Uncle Joseph suggested that I go with him now and Mother and Suzi could join us as soon as their papers cleared. From that moment on, my life became a blur. No one asked me if I wanted to go to America. It was just understood that I was going and I was going alone. In those days, a fifteen-year-old girl wasn't asked what she wanted to do, she was told what she was going to do. I cried. A lot! But quietly so I wouldn't upset Mother. She assured me that as soon as their papers arrived she and Suzi would be close behind me.

Uncle Joseph tried to sweeten the deal by telling me about all the sights we would be seeing on our way. His business would take us to Belgium and France before we took a boat to England. Once there we would travel to Southampton and board the luxury liner "Queen

Elizabeth" for the voyage to America. He made the trip sound like an adventure, and after listening to him I sometimes found myself actually looking forward to it.

Dr. Guckal vaccinated me so I could get my passport. In a few days, the three injections in my upper thigh were swollen and red. The area was infected, but I was a teenager and didn't realize the problem should be attended to. By the time I did, I was too embarrassed to tell my uncle about such a personal thing. I would come to regret this false modesty.

The day finally arrived and Suzi and Mother went with us to the large railroad station in Amsterdam. The train reminded me of the last trip I took alone. This time I couldn't hide the tears. Suzi broke the mood when she clapped her hands in excitement. "Look at the pretty red lamps in the windows," she exclaimed with delight. "Oh, lucky you, Felie. I wish I was going."

After the customary hugs and kisses from Suzi and a cold embrace from Mother, I left for Belgium and America with an uncle I barely knew. Once again I was alone with a virtual stranger and beginning a new life.

The train ride seemed endless, but we finally arrived in Brussels. My uncle was a religious man who observed the Jewish dietary rules. He wouldn't eat in any restaurant that was not "kosher." Of course, it being so soon after the war, no such restaurant could be found. So Uncle Joseph bought eggs and placed them in a small pot of water on top of the radiator in our hotel room. Night after night after night we ate hard-boiled eggs and bread for supper. Sometimes he would buy fresh fruit. But, whenever I said I was hungry, out of Uncle's pocket would come a hard-boiled egg. I was thankful he had at least brought some salt with him.

During the day, Uncle Joseph bought watches he planned to bring back to America to sell. "The profit will pay for our trip, Felie," he explained. He had me wear four or five of them as we passed through Customs.

One day, as we walked through Brussels on our way to board the train for France, Uncle Joseph met a gentleman who seemed to have a lot to say to him. I waited on the sidewalk for what seemed like an hour before they finished their conversation. My uncle finally called me over and introduced me. He told the man he was taking Rosie's daughter to America. It seems the man had lived in the same city as Mother and Uncle Joseph and had even attended Mother and Father's wedding celebration.

"How is Rosie?" the man asked.

"Rosie is fine, " Uncle Joseph answered. "She and her other daughter, Suzi, will be following us to America soon." Then, as an afterthought, he added, "If you ever get to Amsterdam, Leo, make sure you look Rosie up. She'd love to see you."

Leo, a bachelor in his early fifties, was just beginning to get his life in order. During the war, he had walked from Heerlen in South Holland to Belgium and into France where he paid a guide (passour) to lead him over the mountains into Switzerland. He ended up in Montane where he was sent to work on the train line in a work camp. "I worked hard," he told my uncle, "but I survived. Hard work never hurt anyone."

Leo was a three-pack-a-day chain smoker. In order to get his supply of cigarettes and some extra food, he traded diamonds he had smuggled in with him. Before traveling over the mountain, he had swallowed the diamonds to hide them. Once he entered the camp, he kept them hidden by swallowing them over and over again until he needed something. Then he would sell a diamond and use the money for food, cigarettes or anything else he needed.

When the war ended, Leo returned to Holland and settled in Heerlen where he got his factory going again. When we met him, he was coming back from visiting his brother who lived in Brussels. Little did I know that this man with the strong handshake and trustworthy eyes would later marry my mother and become little Suzi's stepfather. I wonder if I would have continued on my journey if I had been able to see into the future.

Uncle Joseph and I left Leo at the station and continued to France and the seashore port of LeHavre where we boarded a boat and crossed the channel to England. I was miserable with seasickness and a fever. But, as sick as I was, I didn't tell my uncle because I didn't want to be a burden. When we arrived in London I was shocked. Most of the buildings and churches had bomb damage and the homes were in shambles. Despite all this, on the day we arrived the city was in an uproar. Princess Elizabeth and Philip had announced their engagement and the British people were thrilled.

Because of the war-time destruction, we had a hard time finding a place to stay for the night. Finally, Uncle Joseph got us one room in a small hotel. The sheets hadn't been changed from the people before us, but we were too tired to look further. Since he realized I was too embarrassed to change with a man in the room, Uncle Joseph offered to go downstairs for a while so I could get ready for bed. I spent most of the time he was gone trying to find something clean that I could use to wash and bind up the festering wounds in my thigh.

The next day we boarded the ocean liner and I was on my way to America. I was placed in a cabin with a single lady I had never met, but I was too timid to complain about that. My fever was worse, and, even though the ship was huge and seemed like a city in itself, my stomach still churned with the motion of the waves.

On our first night out to sea, Uncle Joseph told me
we had been invited to sit at the captain's table. By this
time, I could hardly stand on my infected leg, but I tried
to get dressed anyway. I never made it to dinner. When
my cabin mate came to change her clothes, she found me
on the floor, unconscious. The injection sites were now
three puncture wounds that were as deep as my finger.
The ship's doctor was called and he paged my uncle.
Then he gave me some antibiotics and dressed my
wound.

"Why didn't you tell me you were sick, Felie,"
Uncle Joseph asked. "I can't believe you didn't trust me
enough to tell me about this."

I didn't know what to answer. It was obvious he
hadn't had much experience with shy, fifteen-year-old
girls.

I slept for most of the next three days and four nights
as the ship crossed the ocean. Then, on July 8, 1947, I
joined everyone who had assembled on the deck in the
104 degree heat to ooh and ahh over the Statue of Liberty
as she welcomed us to this country of freedom and
opportunity. Although the war years had torn forty of my
classmates and twelve family members from me and I
was, once again, alone and petrified, I knew in my heart
that God's hand had spared me and He had led me to this
country. It was now up to me to make the most of His
goodness.

Chapter Ten

America is not beautiful like they told me, I thought as I stood on the dock in Manhattan and looked at a view that was far different from what I had expected. *It's ugly!*

The crowd, the noise, the smells—but Uncle Joseph didn't even seem to notice the confusion. He put his fingers in his mouth and whistled as hard as he could. A young boy about eight years old appeared at our side. "This is my son, Marty," Uncle Joseph told me. "Marty, this is Felie, your cousin from Amsterdam."

Marty grinned.

"Why are you wearing long pants?" I asked him. "Is there something wrong with your legs?"

He looked at me as if I were crazy and ignored my question as he started toward the baggage area. He never gave me the chance to explain that in Holland boys didn't wear long pants until they were about thirteen. This child dressed like a man was only one of the many things I saw that day that shocked me as I tried to make some sense out of the strange sounds and sights.

We got our luggage and took a cab to Uncle Joseph and Aunt Hella's home. Another shock! They lived in a gloomy apartment in the basement of a large brownstone building. They owned the building, so, of course, they had rented out all the choice apartments on the upper floors.

Aunt Hella welcomed me and got me settled. Then she handed me something weird—a large chunk of watermelon. I had never seen this food before and didn't know how to eat it, so I watched my cousin Marty. I soon decided that the way to eat watermelon was to pick it up in my hands, eat it fast from side to side, let the juice ooze onto the table in front of me, and then spit the seeds out on the plate. I'm sure my new family wished I had learned my watermelon manners from someone other than Marty. But they say ignorance is bliss, and on that hot day in July I was surely ignorant and not just a little blissful as the cool juice slid down my parched throat.

Cousin Marty's sister was two years older than I. When Doris came home from school, I liked her as soon as I met her. She took one look at me and told her father that we two girls would be going shopping for American clothes and makeup. I had never used makeup, but I thought it was a great idea. So the next day we went to Klein's basement department store in downtown Manhattan. It was the first day of a store-wide sale and I was paralyzed by the confusion. Customers lined up on the sidewalk and when the doors opened, everyone shoved and pushed their way in. I had never seen such a selection of merchandise in my life. People grabbed everything they could get their hands on. It didn't seem to matter if what they captured fit or not. Doris led me by the hand through the chaos, and we came home with bags full of new clothes for me, her happy but exhausted cousin.

I was to stay with Uncle Joseph and his wife for only a few days. Uncle Albert would pick me up on Friday and take me to Long Beach with him where Aunt Sabina and her family were spending the summer. This plan sounded good to me because, although I felt comfortable with this wonderful family in the city, their apartment was dark, hot and humid—a far cry from what I had dreamed America would be.

Friday came. *Would Aunt Sabina and my cousins like me? How would I fit in?* I shivered when I heard the knock on the front door. What a surprise when I opened it. A tall, handsome man with dark, wavy hair stood there. He wore striped pants, a straw hat and a huge smile. "These are for you, Faye," he said as he handed me a huge bouquet of red roses. "Welcome to America." Then he hugged me and kissed me on the cheek and I fell in love with this man and the Americanized name he had just given me.

Uncle Albert was my dashing Clark Gable as he swept me into his large, red car and drove me from the confines of the city to the salty-aired freedom of Long Beach, Long Island where dear Aunt Sabina and her two daughters waited for me.

Aunt Sabina hugged me as she spoke words of welcome in my native language. Her eyes were so much like my mother's that I started to cry. One of my cousins was a little over seven years old and the other was about sixteen months. Seeing their smiling faces made me miss Suzi even more, but their warm acceptance filled my heart with love. They became like sisters to me and we are still that close today.

After I settled in, Aunt Sabina asked if something was wrong. I told her about my leg wounds and she immediately took me to the bedroom to check on them.

"Albert, come here," she cried. "We have to get this girl to the doctor. Now!"

Without a word, Uncle Albert swept me into his arms and carried me down the stairs and down the street to the doctor's house. When we got there, he kicked at the door until the doctor came to open it. Uncle carried me straight through the house to the back room where he finally put me down on a table. The doctor checked me out then sprinkled some antiseptic powder on the wounds and redressed them. "That should take care of the problem, young lady," he said. "This powder works like magic."

Over the next few days the "magic powder" worked and my wounds healed leaving me with three big scars to remind me of my immunization shots and the trip to America.

The family stayed in Long Beach for the summer. Uncle Albert, who I affectionately called *Uncle Abba*, worked in the city and joined us on the weekends. During the day, I enjoyed the beach and my two young cousins, Roslyn and Marian. Then at night, when they were in bed, Aunt Sabina would ask me to tell her stories about the family both before and after the war. Sometimes we would cry over our losses and because Suzi and Mother were not with us. I wrote to Mother every day and when she wrote back her letters spoke of her coming to America and the life we would share when she got here.

When fall arrived, the family moved back to the city where part of our Sunday ritual was for all of us to go downtown to visit Uncle Abba's mother who we affectionately called Grandma Esther. She lived in a basement apartment in a brownstone building where I would often meet three of my cousins. We girls were about the same age and would meet at Grandma Esther's before going out on the town together.

I wasn't too happy that fall when Uncle Albert informed me that since I was under sixteen I had to go back to school. He enrolled me in the Central Needle Trades High School in downtown Manhattan. At first the schoolwork was difficult because, even though I could read and speak English well, writing the language was hard for me. Fortunately, my classmates welcomed me and I soon was quite happy at the school. What a surprise when they voted me the most popular girl at Central

Needle Trades at the end of the term. What a big "to do" at my house!

While in school, I got a job at a small dress store near Aunt Sabina's house. I was paid $1.00 per hour and my boss was pleased with me because I could hem five garments in that hour. At night I would babysit and take my homework with me. The first $5.00 I earned was sent to Mother and Suzi to help them. This pleased Mother so much that she talked about that gift for years after.

My first American major purchase was a Singer portable sewing machine that I bought on credit. The monthly payment was $5.40. When I showed them my official coupon book, my cousins told me I was really getting Americanized: I was wearing makeup, sewing my own clothes, and making time payments.

The first thing I made with my new machine was a felt skirt with poodles on it. This style of skirt was the "new look" at that time, and so I sat on the floor that night and cut out a big circle of colorful felt. Then I folded the circle in fours and cut out a nineteen inch waist. I put in the zipper, appliqued the poodle on front and my new skirt was ready. Extra money from babysitting would buy a blouse for $2.98 and my outfit would be complete.

Each week I gave Aunt Sabina $15.00 for my room and board. Unknown to me, she saved all this money and when I got married she gave me back over $500.00 My husband and I bought our first bedroom set with it.

After graduating from Central Needle Trades, I went to work in a dress factory on Seventh Avenue in the heart of the garment district where I helped to dress the models and take care of the clothes. When there was no fashion show, I would work in the back room examining finished clothes and hand sewing where needed. The factory was owned by a distant cousin who paid low wages. When the unions came in, he told me he didn't want to pay me the higher wage so I would have to leave. I answered a newspaper ad and got a job in a real sweatshop sewing clothes at piece-work wages. The job was in a loft with no fans in the summer. The air was thick with dust from the ripping of the cloth. Since I was quick with my hands, I was able to make about $200.00 per week—an incredible salary for someone who had just come from years of no money, little food, and only one change of clothes. But Uncle Abba was concerned about the atmosphere in the loft and what it would do to my health so he encouraged me to look for other work.

One day, when I was on my lunch hour, I strolled down Fifth Avenue and stopped in front of B. Altmans, a beautiful department store. The clothes in the display window intrigued me and on a whim I went in, found the Personnel Office and applied for a job. They had an opening in the alterations department. The Floor Manager tested me by giving me some sewing to do on a skirt. When I finished, she liked what I had done and hired me on the spot. I was a real American girl now traveling the streets of Manhattan between job and home dressed in the latest styles.

Life was precious to me. I finally had money, but my family and good health were more important. The time spent with my relatives in America slowly began to heal the scars from my war experiences. I started to trust people again, but I was very selective in whom I placed that trust.

The next summer my aunt rented a place at the beach that looked to me like Snow White's cottage in the Disney film. The upstairs rooms were so small that my cousins and I had to sit on the bed when we took off our clothes. If we stood up we couldn't stretch our arms over our heads without bumping the ceiling. I would sometimes sit

on the bed in the early evening and listen to the neighbors
next door as they laughed and talked over the evening
meal. Their joy in being together as a family often made
me cry. I hadn't ever had such companionship with my
parents and now I never would.

I sometimes wonder how my dear Aunt Sabina
tolerated my teenage moodiness and despair. I'm sure
there must have been times when she and Uncle Abba
regreted their offer to take me in. But in the three years
I lived with them, she patiently and lovingly placed
herself in the role of surrogate mother and I soon opened
up to her tender nurturing. She was the mother I had
always dreamed of, and Uncle Abba was the father figure
I had been deprived of. In these two caring people, I
finally found the warm and loving parents I had never
had.

Aunt Sabina played another role in my young
life—matchmaker. The family next door had a son named
Jerry who was about five years older than I was. We
spent hours together commuting on the railroad between
our jobs in the city and our summer cottages. Aunt
Sabina encouraged me to see that "very nice boy" and
that summer Jerry became my best friend. But then the
summer ended. The families returned to their city life and
I was left with loving memories and a heart full of pain
because I was sure I would never see Jerry again. I was
certain of it when I happened to see him kissing another
girl in his backyard just beneath my upstairs bedroom
window.

About two months later, the phone in our city
apartment rang and it was Jerry. "Meet me on Friday?"
he asked, and my heart soared. We met, we walked, we
talked, we reestablished our friendship. That was just the
first of many weekends we spent together throughout that
fall and winter as we enjoyed Broadway shows, good

meals and each other. I fondly remember a double date we had with my cousin Doris, Uncle Joseph's daughter who had been the first to try to Americanize me when I arrived from Holland. We had a wonderful evening full of laughter and good fun. Jerry and I ended up in my aunt's kitchen! Aunt Sabina always made sure she bought Jerry's favorite cakes so that when we returned from our dates he would come in for cake and coffee before starting for home.

When Jerry asked me to marry him, I quickly answered yes. Unfortunately, my joy was dampened by a family disagreement. My aunts and uncles wanted me to have a "religious" wedding performed in a temple. On the other hand, Jerry's parents were Reformed Jews and they did not agree with that plan. After much discussion, Jerry and I decided our love must come before their concerns, so we planned a small wedding ceremony. And on March 26, 1950, we stood before the required number of witnesses in our Rabbi's study. My Aunt Sabina, Uncle Abba, Jerry's brother and sister-in-law, Jerry's mother and father, and my two cousins, Roslyn and Marian, attended.

Once again I was beginning a new life. But this time, I was not alone. My best friend was standing beside me and promising that he would stay with me. With a deeply grateful heart, I thank him for keeping that promise.

Epilogue

At the time of this writing, Jerry and I have been a team for forty-five years. There isn't a day that goes by that I don't thank God for bringing me into the life of this gentle, caring man. His love has helped me to deal with the emotional scars from my wartime experiences and with the deep grief I suffered when we lost dear Aunt Sabina to cancer at the much too young age of fifty-nine. She had not only been there as I adjusted to my new life in America, she had continued to be my support in the early years of my marriage when I was learning to be a wife and yearning to become a mother. She held out hope and encouragement that kept me going through years of infertility, two devastating miscarriages and several surgeries. I truly do not know where I would be today without her.

After six years Jerry and I finally decided to adopt our first child, a daughter we called Nancy. Six years later we adopted our son Edward. They have been a true blessing to both of us.

Mother and Suzi finally received their permission papers, but they never did join me in America. In 1948, Leo Walzer, the gentleman Uncle Joseph and I met in Brussels on our trip to America, went to Amsterdam to establish a factory there. He looked Mother up and they fell in love. Mother always said, "Leo fell in love with Suzi first."

Leo and Mother were married the same year that Jerry and I were. Leo adopted Suzi and it wasn't until she

reached the age of twenty-one and was about to be
married that she was told that he wasn't her biological
father, Siegmund was.

Mother and Leo had twenty wonderful years together
before he died. She lived to the age of eighty-three at
which time she fell at home and broke her hip. During
her recovery, she suffered a stroke which led to a fatal
coma. I knew I had to go to her. Although he wanted to
go with me, Jerry had to stay at home to attend to his
business as a Certified Public Accountant. I flew to
Holland alone and Suzi flew in from Switzerland where
she lived with her two daughters. During the several
weeks we spent at Mother's bedside, I hoped for some
sign of awareness that unfortunately never came.

Mother had never allowed me to tell her how much
I loved her and how I had missed her in my years in
America. Oh, how deeply I had wanted her to come to
live with me and Jerry so I could help heal some of her
war wounds. When Leo died we even built an in-law
apartment for her in our home. She spent a week or two
with us and then abruptly decided that she must go back
to Amsterdam. I was devastated.

Since her death, Suzie and I have spent long hours
talking about the war and the years since. As adult
women, we have a greater compassion for Mother and
can understand her desperate reaching out to the different
men in her life. Each of the men who loved her filled a
need at the time—a need for comfort, economic stability,
and physical security. We have also come to realize that
Mother distanced herself from me emotionally and
physically because I reminded her too much of those
years of pain and the losses she had tried so hard to block
from her mind. She never spoke of her parents, my
father, Siegmond, James, the time with the DeJongs, nor
the family who saved Suzi. She seemed to deal with the

tragedies by ignoring the fact that they had even occurred. Unfortunately, she allowed anger and bitterness to follow her to her grave.

Unlike Mother, I choose to remember. I want this story to bring honor to my loved ones and the multitudes of others who suffered and died. I want the bravery and courage of the Gentiles who risked their lives to help some of us survive to remain on the record. And I especially want mankind to remember what one man with evil design and intent did as he destroyed the lives of millions of innocent people and wrecked havoc on the whole world.

May the recording of these memories prevent such a tragedy from ever being allowed to happen again.

Oma, me and my mother.

Opa Karafiol and me
in 1933.

Susi and me in year 1947
before I left for America.

Me and my mother.

Aunt Sabina and Uncle Abba
who made a home for me in
America and gave me much
love until Sabina passed away
too soon in February 1976.

Me and Uncle Abba,
"My Clark Gable".

Jerry and me at time of our
engagement 1949.

Our dear children,
Nancy (6 $^1/2$) and
Ed (9 months).

Bibliography

Metcalfe, Philip. *1933*. New York: The Permanent Press, 1988.

Sherrow, Victoria. *Cities At War: Amsterdam*. New York: Macmillan Publishing
Company, 1992.

Spiegelman, Art. *Maus: A Survivor's Tale*. New York: Pantheon Books, 1986.

Spiegelman, Art. *Maus II: A Survivor's Tale and Here My Troubles Began*. New York: Pantheon Books, 1991.

Thalmann Rita and Feinerman Emmanuel. *Crystal Night*. London: Thames and Hudson, Ltd, 1974.

Videotape recorded by *Survivors of the SHOAH Visual History Foundation*, P.O. Box 3168, Los Angeles, CA 90078-3168.

Special thanks to
Barbara Robidoux
who edited my writing and
expressed so well
what I intended to say;
and to my dear husband Jerry
for his understanding and help
in bringing to life the dream
that I carried in my heart for so long.

Planted Seed

It took more than fifty years for the "planted seed" from the DeJong's to begin to germinate in me. It wasn't until I got a telephone call from our son Ed when he told us he was going to marry a Christian girl that the seed began to grow.

I was delighted when Ed talked about taking a religious girl for his wife. It made me feel so warm inside, I knew instinctively this was what I had always hoped for.

For years Jerry and I had gone through the motions in observing our religion—mainly celebrating the high holidays at home without going to the temple very often. When we did attend services, they seemed cold since I did not know Hebrew so could not understand the services very well. In our home we had made all the proper attempts to follow the Jewish religion for our children's sake. For a short while, our daughter attended Sunday school. And our son Ed was Barmitzvah'd in what I would call the quick style—that is, without studying Hebrew for a couple of years which was generally required for this ceremony.

So, when Ed, who was now away in the U.S. Air Force, called to tell us Joyce's father had told him he had to become a Christian before he could even go out with her, I was all ears.

As Jerry and I waited to hear how this romance would go next, I found myself thinking back to the evenings around the stove in the DeJong's living room and the Bible study talks came vividly back to me.

Ed took to Christianity like a duck to water. He and Joyce were married and he became a real evangelist to me and

Jerry. At every opportunity he talked to us about the Lord. One time he even said, "My heavenly Father is the only one I have to answer to." For a while that statement did not sit too well with me.

After that, I started to read a small booklet he had sent us about the meaning of becoming a Christian believer. Over the phone we would discuss this for hours at a time. I began to realize the meaning of this and a new warmth enveloped me as we did these readings together.

"Mom," Ed urged, "take the next step. Ask Jesus into your life and ask Him to forgive you of all your sins." Finally, on May 26, 1994, we were again on the phone and I was ready to repeat after him. I asked Jesus to come into my life and forgive me of all my sins. It was so easy! Then Ed said, "Welcome to the family of God."

It did not take long after that (on November 12, 1994) for Jerry to take the step. What a wonderful feeling it was for us to know we were going to heaven together and had received the gift of eternal life!

We began to look for a small church to fulfill our desire to be part of the family of God. We lived in Wilbraham, Massachusetts. at that time. A dear friend told us about the Springfield Church of the Nazarene in the nearby city of Springfield. We went to a Sunday service and fell in love with the wonderful warmth that enfolded us there.

On September 7, 1996, at the lake adjoining our home, the Nazarene pastor, church members, friends, and the Lord watched as we took the next step. On the day of our Baptism, it had rained off and on. But, as we were making our way to Pulpit Rock Pond, the rain suddenly stopped. Jerry and I read our testimonies as the ducks on the lake quacked their applause. Then Pastor Dan baptized us by immersion.

With the Lord, all things are possible. Now, with our new family of God at our side, we feel so blessed.

In the Lord's timing, after twelve years of childlessness, Ed and Joyce had the opportunity to adopt a little boy from Russia. God is so good! Here we are with our roots in Russia and now we have our grandchild from there. I have to believe that Opa and Oma are smiling down at us and little Adam who has completed this beautiful circle of life.

We praise our Lord for our salvation and for His special gift of our beloved grandchild. He truly is an awesome God.

Faye and Jerry